THE MILLION DOLLAR STRIKE

THE MILLION DOLLAR STRIKE

DAN GUTMAN

Hyperion Paperbacks for Children
New York

For information address Hyperion Books for Children, 114 Fifth Avenue, New York, New York 10011-5690.

First Hyperion Paperbacks edition, 2005
This book is set in 12/19 Palatino.
1 3 5 7 9 10 8 6 4 2
Printed in the United States of America
Library of Congress Cataloging-in-Publication Data on file
ISBN 0-7868-1880-8 (tr.) ISBN 0-7868-3751-9 (pbk.)
Visit www.hyperionbooksforchildren.com

Thanks to Woody Woodruff

Dedicated to all the cool kids at schools I visited in 2003:

IN NEW JERSEY

South Mountain School in Millburn; Larchmont School in Mt. Laurel; Marlton and Evans schools in Marlton; P.S. 1 and P.S. 2 in West New York; Hazel Avenue School in West Orange; Denbo School in Browns Mills; Stillman School in Plainfield; McGalliard School in Hamilton; Hubbard School in Ramsey; Travell School in Ridgewood; Barnegat Township School in Barnegat; Woodland School in Warren; Brooklake and Briarwood schools in Florham Park; North Dover School in Toms River; Stockton School in Cherry Hill; Mullen School in Sicklerville; Rush School in Cinnaminson; and Durand School in Vineland

IN ILLINOIS

Avoca West School in Glenview; Baker School in Evanston; Field School in Park Ridge; Braeside, Ravinia, Sherwood, Red Oak, Lincoln, Thomas, Oak Terrace, Indian Trail, and North Shore schools in Highland Park; High Point, Liberty, and Meadow Ridge schools in Orland Park; River View and Meadow View schools in Plainfield; Riley School in Arlington Heights; Sunset Ridge School in Northfield; Hough and Grove schools in Barrington

IN CALIFORNIA

Valley Beth Shalom School in Encino; Stephen S. Wise School in Los Angeles; Buckley School in Sherman Oaks; Crossroads School in Santa Monica; Willows School in Culver City; St. Matthew's School in Pacific Palisades; Cambridge Heights School in Citrus Heights; Del Dayo School in Carmichael; Cowan School in Sacramento

IN IOWA

Four Mile School in Pleasant Hill; Mitchellville School in Mitchellville; Altoona, Centennial, and Willowbrook schools in Altoona

IN PENNSYLVANIA

Radnor School in Radnor; Wayne School in Wayne; Highland School in Abington; Heckman School in Langhorne; Upper Allen, Broad Street, Northside, Filbert, and Shiremanstown schools in Mechanicsburg; Richboro School in Richboro; Blue Bell School in Blue Bell; Goodnoe School in Newtown; Rolling Hills School in Holland; Wrightstown School in Wrightstown; West Rockhill and Sellersville schools in Sellersville; Guth, Seylar, and Deibler schools in Perkasie; Bedminster School in Bedminster; Spring Ridge School in Wyomissing; Devon School in Devon; Gladwyne School in Gladwyne; Merion School in Merion; Grasse School in Hilltown Township

IN VIRGINIA

Oakton and Pine Spring schools in Oakton; Shrevewood School in Falls Church; Cherry Run School in Burke; Willow Springs School in Fairfax; Franconia School in Alexandria; Cardinal Forest School in Springfield; Dranesville School in Herndon; Waynewood School in Alexandria

IN NEW YORK

United Nations International School in New York City; Main Street School in Irvington; Roaring Brook School in Chappaqua; Harrison Avenue School in Harrison

IN ARIZONA

Frontier School in Peoria; North Ranch School in Scottsdale; Lone Mountain School in Cave Creek

IN CONNECTICUT

Davenport Ridge School in Stamford

IN TENNESSEE

Ensworth and Harding schools in Nashville

IN TEXAS

Carroll School in Grapevine; Durham, Johnson, and Eubanks schools in Southlake

CONTENTS

INTRODUCTION

Every story has a beginning, a middle, and an end. That's what Mrs. Felice, my Language Arts teacher, always tells us. She says that every story has a main character the reader can sympathize with. And the main character always changes during the course of the story, so that at the end that character has learned something and has become a better person. Those are the rules of storytelling, according to Mrs. Felice.

Well, I say Mrs. Felice doesn't know what she's talking about.

—Ryan "Ouchie" Miller

CHAPTER 1

Me and Squishy

One pin.

One lousy, stinking, good-for-nothing, stupid pin. It was just standing there, taunting me, mocking me, daring me to knock it over. And I wanted to do just that. I *had* to do just that. For myself. For my dignity. For the win.

"Don't choke, now, Ouchie. I know how difficult these pressure situations can be. One-pin spares are always the hardest to make."

"Shut up, Squishy," I said.

Squishy McFeeters was sitting pretty, having already spared his tenth frame and finishing with a 129, probably the high game of his pathetic bowling life. So he could gloat. Squishy had his feet up on the ball return, hands behind his head, and was leaning his chair back like the game was over and he had finally beaten me. If he hadn't been my best friend since first grade, I'd have hated him.

My grandmother bowls better than Squishy, and when I say that, I don't mean my grandmother is a great bowler or anything. I mean that Squishy is a truly horrible one.

But I had already blown two easy spares, which dragged my pin count down. I had 119 after nine frames. The nine pins I had just knocked down gave me 128. So if I could just knock over this one lousy stinking pin, I would spare the tenth frame, tie Squishy, and give myself one more roll to put him away and shut him up for good. If I missed, of course, Squishy had me, 129 to 128.

One pin.

"You know you're gonna miss, Ouchie." Squishy sighed as I put my hand over the blower to dry off the sweat. "You might as well just pay me the dollar now."

"No way, Squish. You're going down. Like always."

Squishy's dad is a lawyer, which means he has devoted his entire career to arguing with people. Maybe that's why Squishy is so good at it. Maybe that's why Squishy can be so annoying at times—and brilliant at times too.

It was the five pin still standing. That's the one that's right in the middle, directly behind the head pin. It's simple. All you have to do is roll the ball just like your first ball. Nice and easy. Can't miss.

"Staring at it isn't going to make it fall down, Ouch."

My real name is Ryan, but everybody started calling me Ouchie after I dropped a bowling ball on my toe when I was little. I hopped around the alley shouting "Ouchie!" for about ten minutes, and one of the parents caught the whole thing on video. Somehow it made its way to that TV show *America's Funniest Home Videos*, and from that moment on I was Ouchie to just about everyone in Parkfield, California. That's where I live. It's a little town about fifty miles from the Pacific Ocean, between Monterey and Bakersfield. But you don't care about that.

I didn't make up the name *Squishy*. His big brother, Ronnie, did. Ronnie is really overweight, and he used to sit on him all the time when they got into fights. Squishy's real name is Stephen, but the only people who call him that are his parents.

I picked up the ball. It weighs ten pounds. I could probably handle one a little heavier, but this one gives me more control, more accuracy. And right now, I really needed accuracy. I positioned myself at the right side of the lane and brought the ball up to my chest in preparation to begin my approach to the line.

"Hey, Ouch," Squishy said, "wouldn't it be cool if right now some lunatic who escaped from an insane asylum burst in here with a machete and started chasing us around?"

"Shut up, Squish, or I'll make you sniff my bowling shoes."

I wasn't scared. I knew he was just trying to distract me, but I couldn't help but sweep my eyes across the twenty lanes to see if there were any suspicious-looking lunatics lurking around.

Bowl-a-Rama is one of those old-time bowling alleys. They don't have a computer and video screen to keep score for you. You have to do it by hand, on paper. They don't have disco lights and loud music. They don't have "bumper bowling" and they don't do kiddie birthday parties. It's for serious bowlers.

I guess that's why Bowl-a-Rama was just

about empty most of the time. But I kind of liked it that way. No distractions. Except for Squishy, of course.

"Think about it," Squishy continued. "A bowling alley would be a perfect setting for a horror movie. You and I would be the main characters."

Squishy is a horror and science-fiction movie fanatic. Horror is his specialty. He's seen just about every slasher movie ever made. His brain might as well be a horror movie encyclopedia. To Squishy, the real world is just one small step away from a gore film. In his mind, something horrible could happen at any time.

"We're the only ones here, Ouch. It would be so easy for some maniac to leap out from behind that pillar over there and kill us. It would be like that scene in *Night of the Living Dead* when these strangers are trapped in an isolated farmhouse and they get eaten by cannibalistic zombies who were awakened from death by the return of a radioactive space probe."

I figured I might as well just roll the ball. There was no shutting him up.

I focused on the five pin. Didn't have to throw the ball hard. No need to kill the pin. Just have to tap it. If I missed, Squishy would never let me hear the end of it. I could feel the sweat beading up on my forehead.

My dad used to play football at UCLA. This must be what it's like when the clock is ticking down and you're inside the five-yard line and you've got to get the ball past the goal line to score or go home a loser.

I took my approach, brought my arm back nice and easy, slid my right foot forward, and released the ball.

It felt right.

When the ball was halfway down the lane, I could tell it was just a little bit off to the left, but it looked like my shot was still good enough to nick the pin. It was hooking to the left. I just hoped it wouldn't hook too much. It was going to be close.

When the ball was about five feet from the end of the lane, I dropped to my knees in the desperate hope that even if my roll wasn't good enough, I could make that pin drop with a combination of prayer and body English.

I couldn't.

The ball missed by less than an inch. I think the five pin even wobbled a little as the ball blew by it.

"A-ha-ha-ha-ha! In your face, Ouchie!" Squishy shouted as he jumped up and did a little dance. "You owe me a buck!"

I pounded my fist against the foul line. One inch! One lousy, stinking, stupid inch! How could I miss?

Squishy danced his way over to the front desk to return his bowling shoes. I tried to figure out what I had done wrong. Did I twist my wrist too much? Did I rush my delivery?

I was bent over, tying my sneakers, when I sensed a shadow had crept over me. I looked up.

I screamed.

It was the most horrifying thing I had ever seen in my life.

CHAPTER 2

Escape from Bowl-a-Rama

Okay, well maybe I exaggerated just a little. It wasn't the *most* horrifying thing I had ever seen in my life. The most horrifying thing I had ever seen in my life was probably the time I saw Squishy's brother, Ronnie, with no clothes on in the locker room at the town pool. Now, *that* was scary.

But this was pretty terrifying too. The thing that was looming over me was a man. A big man with a big, bushy mustache. He was standing there with a crutch under one arm. The feature that stood out was his bald, shiny head. His head was so shiny, I could see my reflection in it. I could actually see myself on his *head*! It was amazing.

I felt like Darth Vader was standing over me.

The guy leaned his face close to mine and said just four words.

"It . . . was . . . your . . . destiny!"

I opened my mouth to scream again, but I couldn't get my vocal cords working. Nothing came out except for a pathetic frog croak. I hauled out of there before he could grab me.

When Squishy saw me running by the front desk, he dropped the bowling shoes and was right behind me.

"What's wrong?" he asked. "What is it?"

No time to make chitchat. I yanked my bike out of the rack outside Bowl-a-Rama and started pedaling. I didn't stop until we were at my house, where I felt safe enough to tell Squishy what I had seen.

"The guy reminded me of Darth Vader," I said, gasping for breath. I was still shaking.

"Which Darth Vader?" Squishy asked. "Do you mean the Darth in *Star Wars* One, Two, and Three, or the Darth in *Star Wars* Four, Five, and Six?"

"I don't know! This guy walked with a crutch, and he was bald. His head was so shiny I could see myself in it."

Once I had described the guy to Squishy's satisfaction, he told me he thought he knew who I was talking about. He had heard about a crazy bald guy who worked at Bowl-a-Rama, but he had never seen him. I remembered hearing some rumors too. Some people said this bald guy had escaped from a mental asylum. Others claimed he'd had a botched brain transplant that drove him to the brink of insanity. I never gave any of that nonsense a second thought, but Squishy just eats that stuff up.

"Somebody once told me there's a secret machine in the back of Bowl-a-Rama," Squishy said excitedly. "He uses it to kill and torture kids. And he's got a giant safe back there too. He stores the bodies in it until they can be disposed of. I'm telling you, Ouch, the walls of Bowl-a-Rama may be the only witnesses to a horrible secret. And the secret may still live and stalk people."

"Oh, that's crazy," I said, but as he was talking I could feel goose bumps rising on my arms. Who knew what was up with that guy? Maybe he was a murderer. He sure looked terrifying.

"This is the real thing, Ouchie," Squishy whispered. "You and I are part of a horror movie now, and you're the main character. It's just like Mrs. Felice told us in Language Arts. Every story has a beginning, a middle, and an end. This is the beginning, when the evil first shows its face. Then comes the middle, when the evil terrorizes you. And finally, the end, when your character changes for the better, but unfortunately you won't be around to enjoy it, because you have to die."

"Oh, knock it off!" I said, punching him on the arm.

"What do you think he meant when he said, 'It was your destiny'?" Squishy asked.

"Who knows? I wasn't about to stick around to find out."

Squishy couldn't stick around either. He had to go home and eat dinner.

"I'm not going back there, Ouch," he said ominously before pedaling away. "Our sleepy little town may be cursed with an unspeakable evil, a hideous demonic force waiting to spring to fiendish life. As we speak, unsuspecting Parkfield may be harboring a dark and ancient secret so chilling, so frightening, so unrelenting, that nightmares and reality become one. Parkfield may be a town that evil calls home."

"Will you get out of here, Squishy?"

When I went inside, my mom was setting the

kitchen table and my dad was reading the newspaper. Dad is a scientist. He works for a company in San Luis Obispo that tries to predict earthquakes around the world, so he travels a lot for his job.

Mom works at home. She writes articles for *The National Enquirer,* which is that newspaper that they always have near the checkout line in supermarkets. Most of the articles are pictures of celebrities doing stupid things when they don't know there are people taking pictures of them. My mom has a background in psychology, so she usually writes about *why* celebrities do stupid things when they don't know there are people taking pictures of them. My folks are pretty okay, for parents.

"What's that on your pants, Ouchie?" asked my mom. There was a tiny rip on one leg. I must have brushed against something as I was running out of Bowl-a-Rama. Mom notices everything. She had a worried look on her face.

"I probably tore it in the parking lot of the bowling alley," I said. I didn't want to tell my folks about the creepy guy I was running away from. They might tell me to stop going there.

"I wish you would stop going there," my dad

said from behind his newspaper. "I don't like you hanging around that sleazy joint."

Actually, what my dad doesn't like is bowling. He's always trying to get me to play football, like he did. Football toughens you up, Dad always says. Football builds character, he always says.

Yeah, but in bowling nobody tackles you. I never liked the idea of hitting people. And I like the idea of people hitting *me* even less.

"Bowling is my game, Dad," I said, "and Bowl-a-Rama is the only alley in town."

Dad rolled his eyes and returned to his newspaper.

I know a lot of people think bowling is a sport for losers. Or they don't even think it's a sport at all. Most of the kids at school play basketball, hockey, baseball, or soccer. I feel a little funny even telling kids that I bowl three or four times a week. They would think I was weird. But I've always loved the game. I'm not sure why. Maybe because it's the one game I'm pretty good at.

"Listen to this," Dad said, unfolding his newspaper. "It says here that your bowling alley might be closing down."

"What?" I said, grabbing for the paper.

Local bowling alley in the gutter?

PARKFIELD One of the issues to be discussed at Wednesday's town council meeting is whether or not the Bowl-a-Rama bowling alley on Burkwell Road should be condemned.

Bowl-a-Rama has been at its present location since the early 1950s, but in recent years has fallen into disrepair. Several complaints have been filed, some claiming the site is a fire hazard or in violation of safety regulations.

A number of developers have had their eye on this location, looking to tear the bowling alley down and put up retail stores or luxury condominiums, which would bring new life, jobs, and money into the community. However, Gazebo Zamboni, Bowl-a-Rama's owner, has turned down repeated offers to sell. (Continued on page 8.)

"They can't close down Bowl-a-Rama!" I protested, as Dad turned the page.

"They sure can," Dad said, and he went on to

read the rest of the article. "'The town council meeting is open to the public and any interested residents who would like to see Bowl-a-Rama spared (so to speak) are invited to attend.'"

At the bottom of the page there was a photo of Gazebo Zamboni, the owner of Bowl-a-Rama. I leaned over my dad's shoulder to look at the picture. Gazebo Zamboni had a big black mustache and a shiny head.

It was *him*.

CHAPTER 3

The World Behind the Pins

It was hard to concentrate at school the next day. All I could think about was Bowl-a-Rama closing down. I remember going bowling there when I was so small that I had to bend over and push the ball backward between my legs.

There was a new, state-of-the-art bowling alley out on Route 101, but Bowl-a-Rama was the only one I could ride to on my bike. It was *my* bowling alley. I was feeling downright sentimental about the place.

When school let out for the day, I caught up with Squishy riding his bike home. We hadn't had a chance to talk all day.

"Did you hear they might be shutting down Bowl-a-Rama?" I asked.

"Yeah, I heard it on the news last night."

"We should go over there," I said. "You know, to throw one last game for old times sake."

Squishy stopped his bike and looked at me.

"Big mistake, Ouch," he warned. "That guy Zamboni is a psycho killer if I ever heard of one. You don't know what he might be capable of doing. What if you get trapped in there and it's a place where death is the only escape and the victims who die quickly are the lucky ones? Did you ever think about that? What if this Zamboni guy is infected with a virus that will turn him into a bloodsucking, flesh-eating vampire with super-human strength and an appetite for blood?"

"You're nuts!" I told Squishy. "How is he going to kill anybody? He walks with a limp."

"Don't you know *anything*, Ouchie? In horror movies, psychos *always* limp! It's like, a rule. They chase you down some deserted road and it doesn't look like they could possibly catch you, but then you trip over a tree root or something and *bam!* The next thing you know somebody's eating your brains for breakfast."

"Aw, you watch too many of those dumb movies," I said. "Gazebo Zamboni probably won't even be there. You never saw him there before yesterday, did you? Probably somebody else will be working behind the counter today. Come on, come with me. I need somebody to keep me company."

"Me?" Squishy waved me away. "Oh, no. This story is gonna end right here at the beginning. I don't want to see the middle or the end. If I go in there, they'll be carrying my head out in a bowling-ball bag."

"Aw, come on, Squishy! I don't want to bowl alone. Only losers bowl alone. I'm begging you. The least you can do is give me a chance to get revenge for the beating you gave me yesterday."

"I don't know, Ouch . . ."

"What are you gonna do, sit home and work on your homework?" I asked, sneering. "Sit home and study for next week's science test? How exciting! Come on, let's have some fun. I'll buy you a soda."

"Okay, okay!" he finally said. "But I have a bad feeling about this. If that Zamboni guy puts on a hockey mask, I'm out of there."

"Deal."

We ditched our backpacks at my house and rode over to Bowl-a-Rama. The parking lot was empty except for an old yellow Volkswagen Beetle that always seemed to be out there. Somebody must have abandoned it.

There was a sign on the front door of Bowl-a-Rama.

CLOSED.

Hmmm, that's odd, I thought. There was no reason why the bowling alley should be closed on a weekday afternoon. The town council wasn't even going to be meeting until Wednesday. They couldn't have condemned the place already. I tried to look through the glass door, but I couldn't see anything.

"Okay," Squishy said as soon as he saw the sign. "It's closed. Let's go home."

"Maybe they just forgot to turn the sign around," I said, putting my hand on the door handle. "I'm sure it's open."

"Don't open that door!" Squishy shouted, stopping me. "Ouch, if you open that door, I guarantee you, something horrible is going to leap out at us. It might be legions of undead beasts or an army of skeletons or a swarm of genetically altered bats or some other vile, malignant life form. I've seen this happen a million times. Never open doors."

"Oh, stop being such a baby," I said. I pulled the

door handle and it opened. Nothing leaped out at me. There were no monsters or bats or vampires or anything else.

"See?" I said, pulling Squishy inside. "There's nothing to be afraid of."

Right away I could tell something was wrong. All the lights were out except for the ones by the emergency exits. Nobody was around.

"This place reminds me of Camp Crystal Lake in *Friday the 13th,*" Squishy said.

Bowling alleys should be noisy. You should hear the sound of bowling balls crashing into pins and people shouting and laughing. But it was strangely quiet.

"Let's look around," I said, but Squishy grabbed my shirt.

"Are you out of your mind?" he whispered. "It's a creepy deserted building. We saw that bald-headed psycho here yesterday. Can't you put two and two together? You never go exploring creepy deserted buildings with bald-headed psychos in them."

"He's not a psycho," I insisted. "He owns the place. And it's not creepy. It's just dark. Come on. Follow me."

"This is the end of the beginning," Squishy groaned. "Or it could be the beginning of the middle. Whichever it is, something horrible is about to happen. I can feel it."

We made our way past the front desk, being careful not to bang into those big racks filled with bowling balls. I knew from experience that you don't want a bowling ball to fall on your toes.

"I've seen this in a million movies," Squishy whispered behind me. "The smart thing would be for us to turn around and leave right now. But we won't do the smart thing. Kids never do. They always do the dumb thing. And the next thing they know, guys are chasing them around with chain saws or bugs are crawling out of their eye sockets."

"Will you please shut up?" I said. "You're giving me the willies."

The place seemed to be completely deserted. Where could everybody have gone? It was too late for lunch, too early for dinner. I could hear Squishy breathing. He picked up a bowling ball from a rack and held it in front of him, like he was going to bonk somebody over the head with it.

"Do you smell something?" Squishy suddenly asked.

"Yes," I said.

"It's . . . horrible! Ugh! I'm choking! Ouch, we're going to die! It must be . . . poison gas! If I never told you this before, Ouch, you're my best friend. I want you to know that in case this is the end. It smells like death! I'm . . . dying!"

"It's foot odor," I explained. "We're right next to the shoe rentals."

"Oh. Never mind."

"Will you please be quiet now?"

"One of us is going to die a gruesome death here," Squishy whispered. "It will probably be me, because you're the main character and the main character's friend is always the one who gets killed first."

"Does not."

"Does too."

"Maybe *you're* the main character," I said. "Ever think of that?"

"You're right," he said. "No reason why you have to be the main character. I could just as easily be the main character. Then *you* would get killed. Let me lead the way."

I let Squishy go in front of me. But it seemed pointless. Nobody was here. We weren't going to get the chance to bowl. I figured that we might as well go home.

But suddenly, I heard a sound.

It was barely perceptible, but I could tell it was coming from the back of the lanes, behind where the pins stand.

"Did you hear that?" I asked.

"Hear what?"

It was a low, repeating sound, almost like moaning or chanting. It sounded something like . . .

"Nillwob . . . Nillwob . . . "

"Let's get out of here," said Squishy. "Chanting is always a bad sign. People always chant when they're possessed by demons. Did you ever see that scene in *Monkeyshines* when this guy's inner fury is telepathically channeled through his monkey? And then the monkey gets injections of human brain cells and takes control and—"

"Shhhh! It sounds like someone might be hurt," I said. "They might need help."

I walked down one of the lanes, being careful to keep my sneakers in the gutter so I wouldn't mess up the wax on the wood surface. Silently, Squishy followed me, probably because he was too scared to make his way back to the front door by himself.

My eyes had adjusted to the light a little by then. There were pins standing at the end of each lane except one, lane thirteen. I headed in that direction.

"I always wondered what it looks like back behind the pins," I said. "Haven't you?"

"No, never," Squishy replied. "It's lane thirteen, Ouchie! That's bad luck!"

I got down on my hands and knees and crawled through the space at the end of the lane. Squishy crawled through behind me. We had entered . . . the world behind the pins.

"This is the dumbest thing I ever did," Squishy said.

"No, the dumbest thing you ever did was to challenge your brother Ronnie to a baked-bean eating contest."

I half expected and hoped that there would be something magical behind the pins, like in *The Wizard of Oz*, when Dorothy opened the door after the tornado and she was in Munchkinland and suddenly everything was in color.

It turned out that the world behind the pins wasn't all that exciting. There were just some buckets and mops and brooms and stuff.

But the chanting was louder.

"Nillwob . . . Nillwob . . . Nillwob . . ."

We followed the sound down a hallway until it led to a door. Someone was in there. I put my hand on the doorknob.

"Don't open that door!" Squishy whispered urgently.

"Oh, knock it off."

As quietly as possible, I turned the knob and pulled the door open a crack. I put my eye to the opening to see what was inside.

It was Gazebo Zamboni. And he was on the floor.

CHAPTER 4

The Unusual Mr. Zamboni

I jammed my face against the crack in the door, and what I saw was shocking. Gazebo Zamboni was down on his hands and knees in the middle of a small room. He had taken his shoes off. His forehead was touching the floor, as if he were praying. The top of his bald head was touching a silver bowling ball. Both objects were equally shiny. The light from a small lamp next to a bed bounced off his head and was reflected onto the opposite wall. He looked to be about fifty years old, though I always find it hard to tell how old bald guys are.

"I'll bet that's an evil bowling ball with super powers," Squishy whispered in my ear.

Mr. Zamboni's eyes were closed, like he was deep in thought. And he was chanting.

"Nillwob . . . Nillwob . . . Nillwob . . ."

It was very strange and disturbing. I felt like it was something I should not be watching.

"Okay, this is just weird," Squishy whispered. "Let's go home before he tries to recruit us into his bizarre cult of bowling-ball worshipers."

"What do you think he's doing?"

"Maybe he's a Muslim," Squishy said.

"Muslims face Mecca," I told him, "not bowling balls."

The little room was obviously Mr. Zamboni's apartment. He had a refrigerator and sink in the corner. Clothes were draped over a chair and a few pairs of bowling shoes were under the bed. He didn't seem to have any regular shoes. His crutch was leaning against one wall. There was a framed picture of an old lady on the night table.

"That must be his mother," Squishy whispered.

"How do you know?"

"Mass murderers are always obsessed with their mothers," Squishy informed me. "She's probably stuffed and mounted down the basement. That's what the crazy guy did in *Psycho*."

"Shhhhhh!"

There were some old-time record album covers on the floor. I squinted to read the titles. *Wake the*

Dead. Birth of the Dead. Go to Heaven.

"See?" Squishy whispered. "He's obsessed with death. That proves it! He's probably the result of a secret interspecies genetic experiment gone wrong."

"Those are Grateful Dead albums, you moron," I said. "They were an old rock group. My dad used to follow them around the country and go to all their concerts."

"Maybe your dad's a psycho too."

"Shhhhhh!"

We must have made a noise, because suddenly, Gazebo Zamboni opened his eyes and looked straight at us. His gaze was piercing, almost like there were twin laser beams shooting out of his eyes.

"Ahhhhhhhh!" Squishy screamed. I was paralyzed with fear. My legs wouldn't move. Squishy dropped the bowling ball he had been holding. It landed on my toe.

"Owwwwwww!" I yelled. "Cheeeeeee!"

"Holy Toledo!" exclaimed Gazebo Zamboni, getting up from the floor. "Who are *you*?"

"I-I-I'm Ouchie," I said, trembling.

"It's just a story," Squishy moaned to himself.

"It's not really happening." He was holding on to me like I was a life preserver. "Please don't kill us, mister. We didn't do anything. We didn't see anything. We're sorry we interrupted your bizarre bowling ritual."

"Quiet, Squishy!"

"I'm the main character," Squishy said. "So you should kill Ouchie first."

"Kill you?" Mr. Zamboni said. "I should call the police on you boys. You scared the daylights out of me. How did you get in here, anyway?"

"Th-th-th-the door was open," I said. "We heard the bowling alley might be closing and we thought we'd come over and bowl one last game."

"*He* thought we'd bowl one last game," Squishy added. "I had nothing to do with it. I just came along to keep him company."

"You boys were here yesterday, weren't you?"

"Yes."

Mr. Zamboni seemed to soften a bit. He sat down on his bed and pulled on a pair of bowling shoes. Then he came over to us.

"I'm Gazebo Zamboni," he said. "You can call me Mr. Z."

He extended his hand, but Squishy was still

hanging all over me, and I couldn't shake hands.

"There's nothing to be afraid of," Mr. Z said.

"That's what the guy said in *Puppet Master* just before the killer puppet bored a hole in somebody's head and sucked out their brains."

"You live here?" I asked, trying to change the subject. I had finally torn Squishy off me.

"Ten years now. It's the only home I know."

Mr. Z told us that he spent most of his time behind the pins. The ball return and pinspotting machines were constantly breaking down and he was the only one who knew how to fix them. That's why we'd never seen him before. He'd had a few other people to work the desk, but they quit when they heard the news that Bowl-a-Rama might be closing.

"We thought you might be hurt," I said. "You were repeating something over and over again. It sounded like moaning."

"Oh, that," Mr. Z said. "*Gnilwob*. It's *bowling* spelled backward."

I spelled it backward in my head and waited for him to explain why a grown man would be on his hands and knees with his head against a bowling ball chanting *gnilwob*.

"The *G* is silent," Mr. Z said, as if that explained everything.

"Oh, well I guess that's . . . pretty . . . uh . . . normal," I lied.

While Mr. Z turned away to put on a sweater and get his crutch, Squishy whispered to me that in *The Shining*, you kept hearing the word *redrum* and then later you find out that it was *murder* spelled backward.

"This guy is a fruitcake, Ouchie! Let's get out before we get caught up in a bizarre web of circumstances. I'm telling you, if we stick around here, our severed heads will be rolling out of the ball return!"

"Will you please shut up?" I replied.

Mr. Z put his crutch under one arm and made his way slowly to the corner of the room where there was a sink and refrigerator.

"I have something for you," he said, grabbing the handle of the fridge.

"Don't open that door!" Squishy shouted, and then he whispered in my ear, "That's where he keeps the dismembered limbs of the kids he kills! He's going to put *us* in there!"

Mr. Z rolled his eyes. Then he opened the

refrigerator and pulled out three bottles of black cherry soda. He handed one to Squishy and one to me.

"How about joining me for a drink in honor of Bowl-a-Rama?" Mr. Z said, twisting off the cap of his soda and holding the bottle up in the air. "It was a great old bowling alley while it lasted."

"To Bowl-a-Rama," I said, clicking my bottle against Mr. Z's.

"Likewise," said Squishy.

Mr. Z was no longer a stranger to me, so I took a long swig. It tasted good. Squishy watched me before putting the bottle to his lips. I guess he wanted to make sure I didn't start gagging and collapse from the poison that Mr. Z had surely put in the soda.

Mr. Z led us out of his room and back through the winding hallways behind the pins. We didn't have to get down on our hands and knees and crawl through lane thirteen this time. Mr. Z took us a different way.

"Yep, I guess the pins won't be falling at Bowl-a-Rama much longer," Mr. Z said as he made his way to the front desk through the darkness. "Bowling alleys are pretty much like people, I suppose. We're born, we live, and we die."

Squishy shot me a look. Anytime anybody says the word *die,* Squishy shoots me a look.

"Hey, I wonder if they'll bring in one of those big cranes with a wrecking ball hanging from it." Mr. Z chuckled a little bit to himself. "That would be something, wouldn't it? Knocking down a bowling alley with a wrecking ball? That would be appropriate. If I were a bowling alley, that's how I would want to go."

"Isn't there something you can do to keep Bowl-a-Rama open?" I asked.

"Nothing I can do. It's fate. Not many people care about these old dinosaurs anymore. Except for you fellows, of course. Do you still want to roll one last game for old times sake?"

"We'd really like to," Squishy said, "but we should probably get back to the real world."

"We'd love to roll a game!" I said.

"This one's on the house," Mr. Z said. He flipped a switch and the light on lane thirteen went on. The pinspotting machine whirred into action and set up ten pins at the end of the lane.

CHAPTER 5

A Perfect Game

"I still don't trust that guy," Squishy said to me when we went to the rack to pick out bowling balls. "He's trying to make friends with us. You know what that means."

"It means that he wants to be friends?"

"Don't you see, Ouch? They get all palsy-walsy with you in the beginning of the story. They lull you into a false sense of security in the middle. And then, at the end, when they see your guard is down, *bam!* They're chasing you around with really long scissors and you're in a race against time to stop the destruction of all that is alive and real."

"You know what you are, Squish?" I said. "You're paranoid. Why don't you relax for once and enjoy yourself? We're not in a story. There's no beginning or middle or end here. We're not characters and nobody's gonna die. He's just letting us bowl for free."

That made Squishy mad, for some reason.

"You know what you are, Ouch?" Squishy said.

"What?"

"You're totally one-dimensional," he said. "You've got no flaws, no secret past, no enemies, no demons haunting you. You're completely normal. You've got no problems. You're boring. That's why you'll never make a good main character. I would be such a better main character than you."

"Well, then I *do* have a problem," I replied. "My problem is that I have no problems."

"That makes no sense at all, Ouch."

"So what if I'm boring?" I said. "Who says boring people can't be main characters?"

"Mrs. Felice does."

"She doesn't know anything. I say that's discrimination against boring people. It's a total generalization too. And if there's one thing I hate, it's people who generalize."

"Oh, just bowl!" Squishy said.

Mr. Z gave us bowling shoes and took a seat at the table behind lane thirteen. It was the only lane that was lit up. The rest of Bowl-a-Rama was black and gloomy.

"If that light were to go out," Squishy whispered to me as he tied his shoes, "we would be in total darkness."

"Yes," I sighed, "that's pretty much what happens in a windowless room with no lights."

"And that doesn't bother you?"

"Why should it?"

At that moment, I heard a little pop. The light at the end of the lane flickered once, and went out. Everything was black.

"Ahhhhhhhh! We're going to die!" Squishy screamed, grabbing me around the neck. I heard a rustling noise behind me, and then silence.

"Mr. Zamboni?" I said. "Gazebo?"

No answer. I noticed my heart was racing.

"He's gone!" I exclaimed. "Where did he go?"

"He probably went to get some sort of a blunt object. We've got to get out. It's our only hope for survival! This is our chance to escape from his clutches!"

"What clutches?" I said. "Where are we gonna go? I don't know which way the exit is. I can't even see my hand in front of my face."

"I'm so scared, Ouch!"

After a few seconds I saw a pinpoint of light in the distance. It got bigger, and soon I could tell from the way it was swinging back and forth that it was a flashlight. It was moving in our direction.

"He's coming back to get us now!" Squishy whispered. "His evil knows no boundaries! This is it. In case this is the end, Ouch, you were always my best friend. I just want you to know that. I'm sorry I said you were a lousy character. I didn't mean it."

"Okay! Okay!"

Suddenly, all the lights in Bowl-a-Rama went on.

"Blew out a fuse," Mr. Z shouted from the front desk. "Third one this week."

Squishy let go of me. It took a few minutes for my heart rate to return to normal. I picked up my ball casually, as if nothing had happened. I didn't want Mr. Z to know how frightened I had been.

"Okay, let's see what you've got," Mr. Z said, settling into a seat at the table behind us.

I went first. Doing my best to focus on the pins instead of Mr. Z, I rolled a nine, leaving the five pin standing.

Coming back to the ball return, I glanced over to Mr. Z to see if he was going to offer any words of advice. He didn't say anything. I picked up my ball and knocked the five pin down for a spare.

Squishy went up to the lane. "I'm not very good," he announced before turning around to face the pins.

Squishy rolled the ball into the right gutter. Ordinarily, I would have ridiculed him unmercifully. But under the circumstances, I just snickered under my breath. Again, Mr. Z was silent.

I had a pretty decent game, mixing a strike with five or six spares. I ended up with a 135. Squishy bowled horribly and didn't even break 100. He told me he couldn't get comfortable with Mr. Z staring at him with that shiny head and those laser eyes.

The whole time we were bowling, Mr. Z just sat there sipping his soda. He never said a word, never gave us an indication of what he was thinking. It was weird. On the other hand, there was nothing else to distract us from our bowling. The place was empty, it was quiet, and ours was the only lane that was turned on.

Finally, after Squishy finished his tenth frame

with a gutter ball, Mr. Z stood up. We both looked at him with anticipation.

"You," he said, gesturing toward Squishy with his soda bottle. "You need to keep your shoulders square to the foul line. You drop your shoulder and your ball sails wide. It happens because you rush your approach. Keep your back straight. And don't baby the ball. Roll it."

"Yes, sir."

"And you," he said, gesturing in my direction. "You're a tweener. You know what a tweener is?"

"A kid who's not quite a teenager?"

"A tweener is a bowler who's got more accuracy than power. That's a good thing. But it means you get 'No drive, no five.' You know what that means?"

"No."

"It means your ball doesn't drive through the head pin to take out the five pin. That's why you leave it so frequently."

"Is *that* why?"

"You're bending your arm too much at the elbow too. Keep your arm straight and close to your body. Relax your grip on the ball, especially your thumb. Don't squeeze it. And make sure you follow through. After you let go of the ball, your hand should come up to the side of your face. Your release will be weak if you don't follow through correctly."

"Thanks, Mr. Z!"

"Don't mention it. Look, try this," he said. "On your final step up to the line, bend your knee so you get down lower and make sure your right foot doesn't turn as you slide it toward the line. Do it like you're sliding into a deep knee bend. Try that."

"You mean, now?"

"Right now."

I picked up my ball and did as he said. The ball curved smoothly into the pocket and all ten pins exploded out of the way as if a snowplow had run them over.

"Wow," I said. "It worked!"

"Lucky shot," Squishy snorted.

The machine cleared the scattered pins away and set up a new rack. I looked over at Mr. Z. He nodded his head. I picked my ball up and tried to roll it exactly the same way again. And again, I threw a strike. I've always thought that seeing ten pins go down is one of the most beautiful sights in the world, especially when I am the one who knocks them down.

"See what I mean?" Mr. Z said.

I love bowling, but I had never analyzed my game the way Mr. Z did. People don't usually take bowling lessons. They just bowl. But everything Mr. Z said made sense. In a few minutes of his coaching, I probably raised my average by at least twenty pins.

"You really know your stuff," I told him.

"Heck, I hardly told you anything," he said. "You want to hammer the pocket consistently? Someday I'll tell you about rotational energy, spin axis, and radius of gyration."

"Did you used to be a professional bowler?"

"Never bowled in my life," he replied, sitting back down slowly.

"You're joking!"

"Never threw a ball down an alley," he insisted. "Not one."

"Why not?"

"I see it this way," Mr. Z said. "Bowling is the only sport where a person can achieve perfection. A strike is perfection. Ten pins up and ten pins down. If you throw twelve strikes in a row, you've got yourself a perfect game. *Perfect*. A three hundred. That's the magic number. Can't do better than that. Anything less is not perfect."

"So?"

"So I'm working on a perfect game," he said, chuckling. "As long as I don't bowl, I'm perfect. But if I were to throw a ball down one of these alleys and not get a strike, I would be less than perfect. That's why I never bowl."

It did make some sort of sense, in a weird kind of way. I looked over at Squishy. He twirled his index finger around his ear, to let me know he thought Mr. Z was crazy.

"What are you going to do if they shut this place down?" I asked.

"Oh, I don't know," he said. "I guess I'll have a lot of time to kill."

Squishy gulped. "Time to kill?" he said. "Uh, we really have to get going."

"Money won't be a problem," Mr. Z said, ignoring Squishy, "but it will be a shame if they close this joint because I've got something really special in the back, and I won't be able to take it with me if I have to move out."

Squishy and I looked at each other. Really

special? What could that mean? Was it something that was really special, or was it a trap? Really special could mean so many things. Maybe it was that torture device Squishy told me about, or that safe where he stores the bodies. What a tease.

"What's special about it?" I asked.

"It's . . . well . . ." He was at a loss for words. "Would you like to see it?"

"No, thank you!" Squishy said.

"Sure we would!" I said.

"Come with me, boys."

CHAPTER 6

Happy Deathday

Mr. Z was either a genius or he was insane. Or maybe, for all I knew, he was both. The important question was, was he dangerous? Squishy thought so. I doubted it.

My mom once told me that it's not fair to label a person *crazy* or *not crazy*. People are not as simple as that, she said. Some people are completely normal. Some people are unusual. Some are eccentric. Some are weird. Some are nuts, but they're harmless. And some are dangerously nuts—insane.

I figured that Gazebo Zamboni was eccentric. Squishy figured that he was insane. But then, sometimes I think Squishy is insane.

In any case, I decided to follow Mr. Z down the hallway on the side of Bowl-a-Rama. Squishy, who was just as scared of being by himself in

Bowl-a-Rama as he was of Mr. Z, followed me.

Mr. Z led us down a hall I had never seen before. There were all kinds of empty nooks and crannies in the back of Bowl-a-Rama. Mr. Z said there were even some underground tunnels he hadn't explored yet. The hall he was leading us down finally dead-ended at a doorway.

"Don't open that door!" Squishy said, covering his eyes.

Mr. Z opened it anyway and led us inside. The room was dark, but when he flipped on the light we could see a machine that was about ten feet tall. It looked like a big mess of wheels and gears and pumps and bicycle chains. My guess was that it was one of those machines you'd use to milk cows. Squishy guessed that it was "an unstoppable death ray."

"Six thousand parts," Mr. Z said, gazing upon it with what could only be described as love in his eyes. "Two tons. Electromechanical suction technology. She's beautiful, isn't she?"

"Yeah," I said. I had no idea what the thing was.

"Does it work?" I asked.

"No, not anymore."

I saw a blur of movement on the floor. A mouse

or a rat or something scurried out from under the machine. Squishy and I jumped back against the wall. Mr. Z laughed and went around the other side to see if he could catch the thing.

"This must be that machine he uses to torture and kill kids," Squishy whispered in my ear. "It uses that suction technology to suck your brains out."

"It says AMF on it, lamebrain," I said. "That's a bowling company."

Mr. Z came around the other side of the machine. He hadn't been able to catch the mouse.

"This, boys, is one of the first automatic pin-spotters," Mr. Z said, "and it's the last one of its kind left. All the others were thrown away decades ago."

"Cool!" I said, examining the machine.

I had always taken for granted those machines at the end of each lane that set up the pins. But Mr. Z said that ever since bowling was invented by the Egyptians five thousand years ago, somebody had to pick up the pins after each shot and put them back in place by hand. They used to have "pin boys" and "pin girls" who did the job.

But in 1946, Mr. Z told us, a man named

Gottfried Schmidt from Pearl River, New York, invented a machine that swept away the fallen pins and set up a new rack automatically.

"Everybody thought he was crazy," Mr. Z said. "But Schmidt made a fortune when he sold the invention to AMF."

As it turned out, he told us, the automatic pin-spotter revolutionized bowling. The sport spread across the United States and around the world.

"Do you boys believe in ghosts?" Mr. Z asked suddenly.

"No, not really," I said.

"I do," Squishy said. "But I've only seen them in movies."

"Well, I've seen one with my own eyes," Mr. Z told us. "I've seen the ghost of Gottfried Schmidt."

"No way!" said Squishy.

"He comes by here from time to time," Mr. Z continued. "Sometimes, in the middle of the night, when nobody's around, I wake up and hear the sound of a ball rolling down an alley. I rush out and there he is, old Gottfried Schmidt's ghost, throwing one just like he was still alive. He spoke to me once. He told me he was just keeping an eye on his old pinspotting machine. That's what he told me."

"That's *creepy*!" Squishy said.

Mr. Z led us back down the hall. Walking in that direction, we noticed something we hadn't seen the first time. Behind a file cabinet was a safe. It was one of those big safes, about the size of a refrigerator.

Squishy took one look at it and shrank back against the wall, letting out a tortured moan.

"What is it, son?" Mr. Z asked. "Did you see another mouse?"

Squishy could only point at the safe. No words came out of his mouth.

"There's this crazy rumor going around that you kill kids and keep their bodies in a safe," I explained to Mr. Z. "Just ignore him."

Mr. Z let out a laugh. "Is that what people say about me?" he asked. Squishy nodded.

"We don't believe it, of course," I said. "I mean, you would never do anything like that. Would you?"

"Do you want to know what I really keep in here?" Mr. Z asked, taking a large key out of his pocket.

"No," Squishy croaked.

"I'd like to know," I said, "as long as it's not dead bodies."

"I shouldn't be showing you this," Mr. Z said, reaching down to slip the key into the keyhole. "But if it will put your friend at ease . . ."

"Don't open that door!" moaned Squishy.

Mr. Z turned the key and gave the handle a yank. Then he pulled the heavy door open.

The safe was filled with cash. I mean *filled*, top to bottom.

"I call this my wallet," Mr. Z said. He took out a pack of hundred-dollar bills and flicked one side with his thumb like it was a deck of cards. "Whenever I need cash, I just take it out of my wallet."

If all those stacks were hundreds, there had to be millions of dollars in there. Squishy and I just stared at it. I had never seen so much money in one place at one time.

"How did you get all this dough?" Squishy asked.

"I started an online bowling-supply catalog in the early 1990s," Mr. Z told us. "I got lucky. The business took off, and some people bought me out for ten million dollars. Paid me in cash. That was just before the dot-com bubble burst."

Mr. Z told us that he used some of the money to

buy Bowl-a-Rama and stashed the rest in the safe for his living expenses. He doesn't even know for sure how much was left, because he never took the time to count it.

Now, I know for a fact that grown-ups don't manage their money that way. Nobody keeps a bunch of bills sitting around their house. My parents keep some of their money in the bank down the street from us, and they also talk about investments they have in stocks and bonds and mutual funds, whatever those are.

"Lucky I didn't invest it," Mr. Z said. "What with the economy and all, half of it would have been gone by now."

After everything he had told us, I was convinced that Mr. Z may have been a little nutty, but he was not a murderer. In fact, he seemed like a pretty cool guy. I didn't want to see him lose Bowl-a-Rama. With all that money, he could afford a good lawyer. I told him he should fight to keep the bowling alley open.

He shook his head sadly and sat down on one of the chairs near the front desk.

"Do you believe in fate?" he asked us.

"I don't know," I said.

"I never really thought about it," Squishy said.

"Well, I have," Mr. Z said. "I've thought about it a lot. And this is what I decided. Everything that happens in this world is predetermined. Whenever somebody is born or dies, it was determined in advance. If the town council is going to condemn Bowl-a-Rama, then it was fate for Bowl-a-Rama to be condemned. There's nothing I can do about it."

Mr. Z picked up his empty soda bottle and held it up in the air.

"Somewhere," he said, "there's a script that tells us all what to do every minute of our lives. My script told me to pick up this bottle. My script tells me to throw this bottle in that trash can over there . . ."

He tossed the bottle at the trash can about twenty feet away. It bounced off the edge and landed on the floor behind the can.

". . . and my script said I would miss."

"But what if the bottle had gone into the can?" I asked.

"Then I would have a different script," Mr. Z explained.

I tossed my bottle at the trash can and it went in.

"Your script said for you to make that shot," Mr. Z said. "It all comes down to fate, you see."

I thought he was wrong, and I said so. People have always told me that if you try hard enough, you can achieve just about any goal, despite any obstacles. My parents always told me that. So did my teachers. In fact, the whole game of bowling is based on aiming for a target and trying to hit the target.

"If everything in life was determined in advance," I asked, "what would be the point of trying to do anything?"

"There *is* no point," Mr. Z said. "The script tells some of us to try, and some of us to quit. Some of us to succeed, and some of us to fail. But the thing is, none of us know which script we've got until the day we die. Then we're handed a script with the story of our life on it. It's sort of a deathday present. Happy Deathday."

It was suddenly very quiet in Bowl-a-Rama. I didn't like the quiet, and desperately tried to think of something to say to break the silence. But all I could think of was the last thing Mr. Z had said. Happy Deathday. It sounded like one of Squishy's horror movies.

"Well," Mr. Z finally said, "now you know just about all there is to know about me."

"Can I ask just one last question?" Squishy said.

"Of course."

"How do you make your head so shiny?"

Mr. Z got up and led us over to a machine near the front door. It looked a little bit like one of those washing machines with a circular door in the front that lets you watch your clothes go around and around.

"I tinker a bit with inventions myself," he said, getting down on his hands and knees in front of the machine. "I designed this to polish bowling balls. But it has a dual purpose."

He opened the round door and stuck his head inside the hole. Then he reached down with one hand and flipped a switch. The machine rumbled to life.

"It also comes in handy for head polishing!" he shouted, his voice muffled by the noise of the machine. Then he let out an eerie cackling laugh.

Like I said, Gazebo Zamboni was either a genius, or totally out of his mind. One thing for sure—he was part of our story too.

CHAPTER 7

Leslie King and His Posse of Morons

"Today we're going to talk about being passionate," Mrs. Felice told our Language Arts class.

Kids started snickering, because "passionate" sounds like "passion" and "passion" makes people think of love, and anytime anybody says anything that even remotely reminds you of love, you just can't help but snicker.

"Is something funny, Mr. King?"

"No, Mrs. Felice."

Leslie King is this jerky kid who has been in my class every year since second grade or so. He was a jerk then too. One time I remember he stole my hat and played keep-away with it for no other reason than to torment me. He knew I wouldn't fight back, so he just did it. What a jerk.

My mom thinks Leslie King became such a jerk because his parents gave him a girl's name. Apparently, he was named after one of the presidents of the United States, Gerald Ford. Ford's real name was Leslie King. If you don't believe me, go look it up for yourself.

"Everyone is passionate about something," Mrs. Felice said. "What I want to know is, what are *you* passionate about? Mr. King?"

Leslie mumbled something under his breath so Mrs. Felice couldn't hear, but I did. He said, "Richie's mom." Richie was the kid sitting in front of him. Some of the guys sitting around Leslie busted out laughing.

"I didn't hear you, Mr. King. What did you say you are passionate about?"

Leslie stood up at attention and gave a salute to Mrs. Felice.

"Mrs. Felice, I am passionate about BMX biking," he said in a robotic military voice. "That is trick biking, ma'am, and when I grow up I plan to become a trick biker."

"Very admirable," Mrs. Felice said.

Leslie saluted again and sat down. I've got to hand it to him. He knows exactly how to play the teacher and at the same time make his posse of morons think he's making fun of the teacher. That's not easy.

"What about you, Lindsay? What are you passionate about?"

"Cheerleading."

"Good. And what about you, Jessica?"

"Playing the piano."

"And you, Mr. McFeeters?"

Squishy stood up. "Horror movies," he said, to the accompaniment of a few giggles.

"Oh, and what is it about horror movies that you find so interesting?"

"I kind of like being scared."

"I see."

Mrs. Felice had us go around the room saying what we were passionate about. Some kids said normal things like soccer or horseback riding. Whenever anybody said something a little unusual, like poetry or going to museums, Leslie and his posse of morons would snort and cackle.

I wasn't sure what to say. I wanted to say something that would make the other kids think I was cool, but I really wasn't passionate about anything that other kids think is cool. There was really only one thing I was truly passionate about, and that was bowling.

"Bowling," I said, when it was my turn. Leslie let out a loud snort, and I thought that would be the end of it.

"Okay, your assignment for tonight," Mrs. Felice told us, "is to write a two-hundred-word essay on that one thing you are passionate about. Be thoughtful, be descriptive, show me some metaphors and similes. And *please* check your spelling, because you know I will."

"Can we write more than two hundred words if we want to?" asked Jessica. She always wants to do more than the teacher asks for, the little brownnoser.

"Of course, Jessica."

"Can we write less than two hundred words if we want to?" asked Leslie King.

"Well," Mrs. Felice said, "if your essay is well written but comes in at a hundred ninety-eight words, you won't lose points."

"What if it comes in at ten words?" Leslie mumbled, too low for Mrs. Felice to hear, but loud enough for his posse of morons to laugh at.

I spent about an hour that night composing my essay. This is what I wrote. . . .

Bowling: The Perfect Game

In just about every sport, you aim for a target. In football, the kicker has to kick the ball through the goal posts. In basketball, you have to throw it through a hoop. In hockey and soccer, you have to aim for a net. While aiming for a target is a part of all these games, in bowling aiming for a target is the whole game. That's why I'm passionate about bowling.

I think human beings like to aim for a target and try to hit it. We are goal-oriented creatures.

It could be said that bowling is a metaphor for life. In life, we like to set goals (like targets) for ourselves and try to achieve (hit) them. The pins are my goal and when I knock them down, I have achieved my goal. There's no better feeling.

The other thing I like about bowling is that it is the only game that lets you achieve perfection. I mean, a baseball pitcher can throw "a perfect game," but it's not really perfect. He threw some pitches out of the strike zone. Some of the batters hit the ball. But if you bowl a perfect game, you were perfect. Twelve rolls, twelve strikes: 300 points. I may never achieve it, but my goal in life, and in bowling, is to one day roll a perfect game.

I thought my essay was pretty good. The first draft was a little short, so I added that last paragraph about rolling a perfect game. In the end, it came out to 226 words.

Mrs. Felice doesn't usually read our work out loud, but she must have really liked my essay. It was the only one she read to the class. I was embarrassed, of course, and I slunk down a little in my seat because I knew everybody was looking at me.

The whole time Mrs. Felice was reading my essay, Leslie King and his posse of morons were cackling and making rude comments to each other. When he knew she couldn't see him, Leslie stood up and did a stupid impersonation of somebody bowling.

"Hey, Ouchie," Leslie whispered. "Did you know that if you add the letter *E* to *bowl*, it spells *bowel*? Did you ever go bowling and have a bowel movement?"

That's Leslie's idea of humor. Well, his posse of morons thought that adding an *E* to *bowl* was just about the funniest thing they had ever heard in their lives. They were falling off their chairs, and Mrs. Felice ended up sending a few of them to the office. Served them right.

Mrs. Felice gave me an A and told me she liked that way I had used a metaphor in my writing.

After school, Squishy and I were riding our bikes home together, like always.

"Hey, bowel boy!" a voice yelled from behind me on the sidewalk. I knew right away it was Leslie King. Turning around, I could see he and his posse of morons were pedaling hard to catch up to me and Squishy.

I ignored him. I knew that if I tried to get away, they would catch us. If I stopped, I would be asking for trouble. Maybe if I just pretended he wasn't there he would leave me alone.

"Just be cool," I told Squishy.

"Hey, bowel boy!" Leslie said. He was coming up alongside me on the left.

"What?" I asked, refusing to look at him.

"Do you get a lot of strikes?"

"Every so often," I said.

"Well, here's another one," Leslie said, and he reached out and punched me in the ribs. "Ha-ha-ha-ha!"

I wanted to pretend it didn't hurt, but it did. My side was killing me. I had to stop and catch my breath. Leslie and his posse of cackling morons surrounded me on the sidewalk. I looked around for Squishy. He had stopped about fifteen feet behind me. He was looking the other way, like he didn't want to get involved. Big help.

"Hey, bowel boy, did you ever throw a perfect game?"

"No," I said, holding my side. It hurt pretty bad, and I was afraid he might punch me there again.

"Of course you didn't," Leslie said. "Nobody's perfect. Every once in a while you throw one in the gutter, right?"

With that, he reached out and gave me a shove. I wasn't expecting it. I fell to my right and the weight of my backpack carried me off my bike and I landed on the curb.

"Ha-ha-ha-ha-ha-ha!"

Leslie and his posse of morons pedaled away, laughing the whole way down the street.

I was okay. My backpack was in the gutter and some of my books had fallen out of it, but my bike wasn't damaged and neither was I.

I was picking my stuff up when Squishy finally came over. He picked up my bike for me.

"You're gonna help me *now*?" I yelled at him.

"I would have helped, Ouch, but it all happened so fast and by the time I—"

"No buts," I hollered at him. "You bailed on me! You should have been with me when they were harassing me. I don't need any help *now*. What was all that crap about being best friends? Some friend *you* are."

"I'm sorry, Ouchie. I was afraid he was going to go after me next."

"Maybe he *will* go after you next," I said. "Don't expect any help from me. Thanks a lot. Thanks for nothing."

I rode the rest of the way home by myself.

CHAPTER 8

The Fate of Bowl-a-Rama

That night, Wednesday, was the day for the monthly town council meeting, when the mayor and all the local big shots get together to talk about stuff affecting the town. I went to one once. There had been some traffic accidents on our street, and my dad wanted the town to put up a stop sign at the end of the block. It was really boring to listen to the politicians talking, but in the end they did agree to put up that stop sign.

I had decided to go, because I knew that one of the things they were going to vote on was whether or not Bowl-a-Rama should be condemned. I didn't bother calling Squishy to ask him if he wanted to come with me. I was still mad at him because he hadn't helped me when that jerk Leslie was hassling me.

The meeting had already started when I arrived at the municipal building. The members of the town council were sitting at a long table at the front of the room. The mayor, Liza Little, was in the middle. She was the first female mayor in Parkfield history. Chief of Police Fender Stratocaster was at the table too. I knew him because he comes to our school all the time to talk about smoking and drinking and drugs and stuff. All the kids call him Chief Strat. There were about twenty people in the audience. I looked around for Mr. Z, but he wasn't there.

They went on and on about the town sewers for a while, and then Mayor Little pounded her gavel and said it was time to discuss "the Bowl-a-Rama situation."

I didn't know the names of the people on the town council, but one by one they spoke. I just sat there and listened.

"That bowling alley is an eyesore."

"Nobody ever goes there. I wouldn't take my kids there. Would you?"

"It makes our whole town look seedy."

"Never mind all that," Police Chief Strat said. "Bowl-a-Rama is an accident waiting to happen.

No improvements have been made in fifty years. The building is not up to code. The whole place could collapse or burn down any minute. What if somebody gets injured in there? Is the place even properly insured? I say we condemn the place now, before something happens."

"Bowling is so low class anyway."

"That's not true!" shouted a man in the back. Everybody turned around to look at him. He got up, indignantly. At last, somebody was going to defend Bowl-a-Rama.

"Who are you, sir?" asked the mayor.

"My name is Cliff Dweller, and I own the new Bowl Drome bowling alley on Route 101. Bowling is *not* low class. But run-down old bowling alleys like Bowl-a-Rama make it *look* low class. That Zamboni fellow hurts the whole image of bowling, and he's hurting my business. That's why I want you to shut him down."

"I would bet that a big corporation like Wal-Mart or Burger King would love to have that location," said some guy in a suit. "And that would provide jobs to revitalize our community."

Another angry guy in the audience stood up and demanded to speak.

"We don't need another Burger King!" he said. "Don't we kill enough cows every day as it is? And those faceless burger chains are ruining the distinctive character of small-town America."

"And who are *you*, sir?" asked the mayor.

"My name is Herb Dunn. I'm a member of PETA, which stands for People for the Ethical Treatment of Animals."

"I know what it stands for," said the mayor. "And what do *you* propose we do with this location, Mr. Dunn?"

"I would like to buy that land and open up a dog bakery," he said.

"You're want to bake *dogs*?" Chief Strat asked. "That's disgusting!"

"No, I bake all-natural gourmet food for people to *buy* for their dogs. Little doggie cakes and muffins, things like that."

"Let 'em eat Alpo!" somebody shouted from the audience. "I'd rather have a Burger King."

Everybody started laughing and talking to each other until the mayor pounded her gavel and shouted, "Order! Order!"

I looked around the room. I would have thought somebody would stand up and say Parkfield needed to keep its only bowling alley, but nobody did. I wanted to get up and say what was on my mind, but I was scared. I was the only kid in a sea of grown-ups.

They kept droning on and on, trashing Bowl-a-Rama, when somebody slid into the seat next to me. I turned around and was shocked to see that it was Squishy.

"Hey, wouldn't it be cool if a flesh-eating army of walking corpses came in right now," Squishy whispered, "and they ate the entire town council?"

"Yeah, that would be cool," I said, slapping Squishy's hand.

Somehow, having Squishy beside me gave me a jolt of confidence. I got up from my seat and raised my hand. It was a while before the mayor noticed me.

"May I say something, please?" I said.

"Of course," Mayor Little said. "We always like to see our young people get involved in the issues confronting our community."

I knew that was a lot of bull. A few years ago some of the kids at school circulated a petition to get Parkfield to build a skate park, and the town council basically told them to get lost.

"I think it would be a big mistake to tear down Bowl-a-Rama," I said. Everybody in the room turned to look at me, and immediately I started sweating.

"You tell 'em, Ouchie," Squishy whispered.

"Why would it be a mistake, son?" the fire marshall asked.

"Bowl-a-Rama is historic," I said. "Did you know that the world's first mechanical pinspotter is there? It revolutionized the sport of bowling."

"What the heck is a pinspotter?" Chief Strat asked. A few grown-ups laughed.

"It's the machine that picks up the pins that get knocked over and sets up new ones," I said. "We've got the first one right here in Parkfield. Instead of tearing Bowl-a-Rama down, you should be talking about fixing it up and putting a plaque out front to let people know we have something famous in our town. It should be a national landmark."

There was a buzz around the room. I was starting to regain my confidence.

"To condemn Bowl-a-Rama would be like condemning the Wright brothers' first airplane just because it was old," I continued. "It would be like condemning Edison's first lightbulb or Eli Whitney's first cotton gin."

The members of the town council must have thought that was funny. They were chuckling among themselves.

"You should have quit while you were ahead," Squishy told me.

"I hardly think it's fair to equate the lightbulb and the airplane to some bowling gizmo," said Mayor Little. "And if that pinsetter or whatever you call it was such an important invention, why isn't Gazebo Zamboni here to say so himself?"

"Yeah!" a few people agreed.

I knew why Mr. Z wasn't there. He thought everything came down to fate. He didn't believe that fighting for what's right would do any good because his "script" said Bowl-a-Rama was going to be condemned no matter what.

I couldn't say that, of course, because then they would all think Mr. Z was crazier than I thought he was.

"I've heard rumors about this Zamboni fellow," Chief Strat said. "Vicious rumors."

"Those rumors are lies!" I yelled.

"I propose we put it to a vote," Mayor Little

said. "All in favor of condemning Bowl-a-Rama, raise your hand."

Every single member of the town council put a hand up.

"Well, then I believe we are unanimous," Mayor Little said. She picked up her gavel. But before she was able to pound it down, Squishy jumped to his feet next to me.

"I say it's prejudice!" he shouted. "That's what I say!"

A hush fell over the room as everybody turned around to look at Squishy.

"And who are *you*?" Mayor Little asked, squinting into the audience.

"My name is Stephen McFeeters, and I have lived in Parkfield all my life."

"Yeah, and he's my friend too!" I added.

Squishy walked up to the town council in the front of the room. He looked like one of those lawyers you see on TV who goes and talks to the jury. He must have picked that up from his dad.

"I think we all know what's going on here," Squishy said. "Gazebo Zamboni is one of the few Italian American business owners in this town, and you don't like that. Why don't you come out and admit the *real* reason you want to condemn Bowl-a-Rama? You're prejudiced against minority groups!"

Some people in the audience gasped. All the big shots on the town council sat back in their seats, stunned and outraged.

"That's preposterous!" claimed the mayor. "I don't have a prejudiced bone in my body."

"Oh, yeah?" Squishy said. "That may be true. But I say your ligaments and tendons are prejudiced against Italians!"

Everybody in the room gasped again, including me. I didn't know Squishy had it in him.

"Italians aren't a minority group," the guy in the suit said.

"Sure they are," said somebody else.

"That was brilliant!" I whispered when Squishy came back to his seat.

"I owed you, Ouchie. I'm sorry about the bike thing."

I stood up. "Mr. Zamboni is handicapped!" I shouted. "I suppose you're trying to run cripples out of town too."

The members of the town council buzzed among themselves for a few minutes until Mayor

Little pounded the gavel and demanded quiet.

"I propose we give Bowl-a-Rama thirty days to get its act together," the mayor said. "If, in our judgment, it is still a blight on our community at that time, we will shut it down permanently. All in favor?"

Everybody on the town council raised their hands.

"Meeting adjourned."

CHAPTER 9

Going Out with a Bang

The next day, I was in such a good mood. Squishy and I were friends again. We had convinced the town council to give Bowl-a-Rama a month to fix itself up. And to top things off, that jerk Leslie King was absent from school. Now, *that's* a perfect day.

After school, Squishy and I rode our bikes over to Bowl-a-Rama to deliver the good news. Along the way, I got Squishy to admit to me that he had been all wrong about Mr. Z. He didn't murder kids and stuff their bodies into a safe in the back room. He was just an odd guy who polished his head and talked with ghosts and wore bowling shoes all the time, that's all.

"Okay, okay, maybe we're not in a horror movie after all," Squishy admitted.

We skidded into the parking lot, which was

empty as usual, except for that yellow Volkswagen Beetle that was always parked in the corner. We were about to go into Bowl-a-Rama when Squishy noticed somebody was sitting in the driver's seat of the Beetle. I always thought that car had been abandoned, but when we went over to check it out, we could see that the person was slumped over the steering wheel.

"It's Mr. Z!" Squishy shouted as we got closer. "And he's dead!"

We ran to the car, and found that Mr. Z wasn't actually dead. He was sobbing, tears running down his face.

"What is it?" I asked. "Are you okay?"

"It's all over," he sobbed.

"No it's not," Squishy said. "We went to the town council meeting last night. Everything's going to be okay."

"Boys," he said, turning to face us, "it doesn't matter what happens to Bowl-a-Rama. The world is going to end on December thirty-first."

"What?"

"I saw the ghost of Gottfried Schmidt again last night," Mr. Z said. "He's really angry."

Squishy and I looked at each other.

"The plot thickens!" Squishy said gleefully.

"What's this ghost angry about?" I asked.

"He doesn't like what's happened to bowling since he died," Mr. Z said. "He doesn't like the lights and lasers and music and all that. He says it destroys the essence of the game. To punish us, he's going to destroy the world. Just knock it down like a rack of bowling pins. And he is going to do it on New Year's Eve. That's what he told me."

Squishy and I looked at each other again. Mr. Z may have been crazier than I thought. Maybe he was getting worse. Maybe he needed help.

Then he handed me an envelope.

"I was about to go out and pick up some groceries," he said, "when I found this under my windshield wiper."

I opened the envelope and this was inside it:

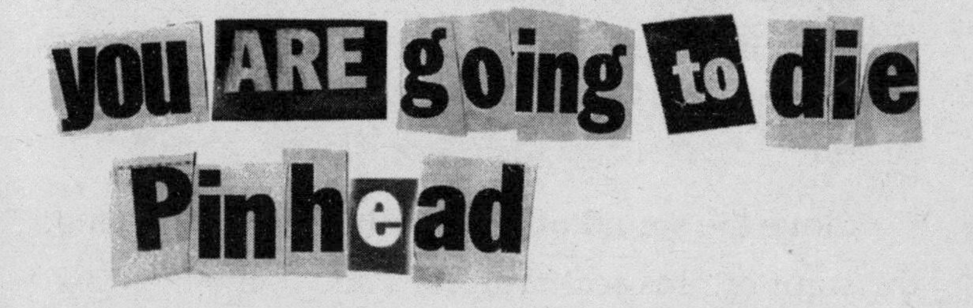

"It's just a prank," I said. "Some obnoxious kids must have left this here."

"I don't think it's a prank, Ouch," Squishy said. "Somebody went through a lot of trouble to make this. They cut out all the letters so their handwriting wouldn't give them away."

"Do you have any enemies?" I asked Mr. Z.

"No. It's from the ghost of Gottfried Schmidt," Mr. Z said slowly. "He wanted me to have it in writing. This is my invitation to the end of the world."

"The world is *not* going to end!" I said firmly. I stuffed the note in my pocket.

But Mr. Z wasn't listening. He just sat there, staring out the windshield.

"If only life could be as simple as bowling," he said, as if he were in a trance. "You roll a ball and knock the pins down. The machine puts the pins up again, and you knock them down again. So simple. Life, on the other hand, is so complicated."

"He's hallucinating," Squishy whispered in my ear.

"I love the sound of a ball rolling down the lane, the sight of pins scattering. It's so . . . final," Mr. Z muttered. "I love the smell of bowling-alley wax in the morning."

"We've got to get him help," I told Squishy. "He's losing his marbles."

I didn't quite know what to do. It was almost like Mr. Z was going crazy right before our eyes.

"What about that threatening note?" Squishy said as we pedaled furiously to my house. "He didn't hallucinate *that*. Somebody wants him dead."

"He's going psycho," I said. "Right now, he needs a psychologist or a psychiatrist or a psychotherapist or something."

"Isn't your mom a psychologist?"

"She majored in psychology in college," I told him. "She writes articles about psychology for *The National Enquirer*."

"Same diff."

My dad was out of town, as usual. There was an earthquake in Turkey and he had to go there and see the devastation in person. But Mom was home, working at her computer.

"Mom!" I hollered as soon as we ran in the door. "You've got to come to Bowl-a-Rama with us right away! Mr. Z is having a meltdown!"

"I'm on deadline," she said. I knew my mom

was working on a big story about a guy in Texas who claimed he'd found Hitler's brain in a pickle jar in his garage. "What is it?"

We sat down and told her everything about Mr. Z. How he lived in the back of the bowling alley and prayed to bowling balls. How he refused to bowl because it would ruin his perfect game. How he talked with the ghost of Gottfried Schmidt. How he thought the world was going to end. How he stuck his head in the ball-polishing machine.

"I don't like you hanging around with this man," she said. "He might be dangerous. Maybe we should call the police."

"But he's harmless, Mom! He wouldn't hurt a fly. You've got to trust me on this. Mr. Z doesn't need to be arrested. He needs help."

Mom thought it over for a minute or so, and then she snapped her fingers.

"Bowlaphobia!" she exclaimed.

"Huh?"

"The solution is simple," Mom said. "Mr. Zamboni doesn't need therapy. He just needs to *bowl.*"

"How do you figure that?"

"It's obvious that Mr. Zamboni is hung up on

the concept of the perfect game," Mom said. "He sees that the world around him isn't perfect, so he shrinks into his own, limited, perfect little world."

"Why would bowling cure that?" Squishy asked.

"Don't you see? Once he bowls and gets less than a strike, he'll realize that the world is no different from before. Nobody's perfect. He wasn't perfect *before* he bowled, and he won't be perfect *after* he bowls, regardless of how many pins he knocks down. He'll see that whether or not somebody bowls has no bearing on how good a person they are. A whole new world will open up to him once he gets past his . . . fear of bowling."

"Bowlaphobia!" Squishy shouted.

"You're a genius, Mom!" I said, giving her a hug. I'm so lucky to have a mother who is an expert in human behavior.

"It's just basic psychology," she said, turning back to her story about Hitler's brain.

Squishy and I rushed back to Bowl-a-Rama. I hoped we weren't too late. Mr. Z had looked so depressed when we left him in the parking lot, I was afraid he might drive his Volkswagen over a cliff or something.

When we got to the bowling alley, the Beetle was still in the parking lot, but it was empty. Breathlessly, we rushed inside Bowl-a-Rama. Mr. Z was on his hands and knees, polishing his head in the ball buffer.

"Oh, hello, boys!" he said when he was done. He looked like he was back to normal. Well, normal for *him*, anyway.

"We need to talk to you about something really important," I said.

"What is it?"

"We want you to bowl," Squishy said. "We think you would be a lot happier if you bowled."

"What makes you think I'm unhappy?" Mr. Z said cheerfully. "I'm perfectly happy. I've never been so happy in my life. I'm deliriously happy."

"You weren't very happy fifteen minutes ago," Squishy said.

"That was fifteen minutes ago," he told us. "Nobody's happy all the time."

"But just think how much happier you would be if you bowled," I suggested.

"Nothing could make me happier," he replied. "In a few short weeks, all my troubles will all be over. The world will come to an end and life as we know it will screech to a halt. That's what Gottfried told me. I can hardly wait. The tenth frame is almost here. Why should I screw up my perfect game by bowling *now*?"

Mr. Z wasn't better. He was just coping with his sickness in a different way. My mother hadn't told me what to do if he reacted like that.

How can you force a guy to bowl? What were we going to do, put a gun to his head and say, *We have ways of making you bowl*? I was getting desperate, angry even.

"You *never* want to bowl," I said, raising my voice a little. "But *we* do. Did you ever think of that? If Bowl-a-Rama shuts down, we'll have no place to bowl. Parkfield will be bowling alley–less. How will *that* be good for bowling? If people come to this very spot and there's a Wal-Mart or some dog bakery, how is *that* going to be good for bowling? You should fight to keep Bowl-a-Rama open for the sake of the kids like us, and future generations of bowlers."

Mr. Z just smiled and shook his head.

"After New Year's, there won't *be* a future generation of bowlers."

Squishy excused us and pulled me off to the

side. "Will you be quiet already?" he whispered. "The more you talk, the worse off we are. Let me do the talking. I have an idea."

We went back to Mr. Z, who was sweeping the floor with a broom.

"I was thinking," Squishy said, "seeing as how the world is going to end on New Year's Eve and all, wouldn't it be cool to go out with a bang?"

"What do you mean, go out with a bang?" Mr. Z replied.

"You know, we could fix this place up nice and throw a big End of the World party," Squishy suggested. "We could get some music, cool lights, food, and invite the whole town. I mean, it's all going to be destroyed anyway. What difference would it make at this point? Everything comes down to fate, right?"

A light seemed to glow in Mr. Z's eyes.

"Go out with a bang," he said with a glassy-eyed smile. "I like that idea."

"Sure you do," Squishy said, throwing me a wink that surely meant, *See? All psychos like to go out with a bang.*

"Music and lights and food and all that other stuff will cost a lot of money," I said. Squishy shot me another look. This one said, *Shut up*.

"I'll take the money out of my wallet," Mr. Z said. "You can't take it with you. That's what they say, right?"

"That's exactly what they say," Squishy agreed. "You might as well enjoy your money while you're alive, because it won't do you any good when you're dead."

"Go out with a bang," Mr. Z repeated. "Yes, perhaps *that* is my destiny."

CHAPTER 10

The Makeover

If Mr. Z didn't want to try and save Bowl-a-Rama, Squishy and I decided that we would try to save it ourselves. Maybe, in the process, we would save Mr. Z too.

I have to give credit to Squishy, who is truly a genius. If it were up to me, I would have kept trying to prove to Mr. Z that the world wasn't really going to end on New Year's Eve. But Squishy turned the whole thing around by pretending Mr. Z was right. If he truly thought the world was going to end, it wouldn't matter to him if we fixed up Bowl-a-Rama.

"Do whatever you want to the place," he told us. "Knock yourselves out. It'll all be over soon anyway."

If we needed any money, he told us, all we had

to do was let him know, and he would take it out of his "wallet."

Squishy and I sat down and decided we were going to take shabby old Bowl-a-Rama and turn it into the coolest, most fun, state-of-the-art bowling alley in the world. To do that, we would have to make a visit to the bowling alley more exciting than going to a movie, a ball game, concert, or anything else.

We didn't exactly know where to start, so we just picked up the phone book, turned to *Bowling*, and started dialing numbers.

The first thing we did was order these awesome glow-in-the-dark bowling shoes and Day-Glo bowling balls. They arrived a few days later, and instantly the place looked cooler than it had looked the day before. We took all the old junky scratched-up black balls outside and lined the edges of the parking lot with them. Inside, they looked terrible. But outside, they looked awesome.

We chose some funky bowling posters for the walls. We had all the lanes refinished. We pulled out all the puke-colored carpet (probably colored with real puke) and put in new carpet with bright colors. We bought computers for each lane that not only kept score for you but even offered tips on the best way to make your spares, left-handed and right-handed.

Next, we ordered two of those rotating mirror disco balls and a colored laser system so we could turn off all the regular lights and make the place look like a nightclub. We ordered the biggest sound system available too, so we could blast music at eardrum-piercing levels.

We ordered pool tables and the hottest new arcade video games. We installed big-screen TVs all over the place, so people could have something to watch while they were waiting their turn to bowl.

When the delivery men showed up with all this stuff we had bought, they couldn't believe that a couple of thirteen-year-old kids had the authority and the money to order it. We would just call Mr. Z over. He'd pull out a stack of those hundred-dollar bills, and their eyes would light up. They would do anything we told them.

Spending money is fun, especially when it's somebody else's money. We hired landscapers to plant bushes out front and to trim them in the shape of giant bowling balls and pins. We brought in one of those gourmet coffee companies to open up a little kiosk so people could have a cappuccino or one of those other awful-tasting drinks grown-ups like while they bowled. We installed some Internet terminals so bowlers would be able to surf the Web or check their e-mail between games.

While all this was going on, Mr. Z would walk around watching all the hubbub. We kept thinking he was going to tell us to stop. We thought he would complain that we were ruining the essence of bowling. But he never did. He'd just shake his head and laugh.

"It all comes down to fate, right, Mr. Z?" Squishy kept saying.

"Right!"

Mr. Z actually seemed relatively sane for once. He didn't mention any ghosts, and we didn't see him praying before bowling balls or anything. Maybe this whole bowling alley makeover was doing him some good.

It was doing Squishy some good too, I noticed. He didn't spend every waking minute fantasizing about homicidal maniacs who were about to kill us and man-eating spiders and things like that. He threw himself into the work. The two of us would rush over to Bowl-a-Rama after school every day to supervise.

We were spending a fortune, and I was starting to feel funny about it. I was starting to think that maybe we were taking advantage of Mr. Z. After all, the guy was borderline crazy. Was it really right for us to dupe him into spending all this money? Was he sane enough to make this decision for himself? Were we in some way encouraging his insanity?

Squishy and I talked it over. Mr. Z didn't have any children, so it wasn't like we were spending anybody's inheritance or anything. If we didn't do what we were doing, the town was going to tear Bowl-a-Rama down. Where would that leave Mr. Z then? We were saving the one thing that was important to him.

After much discussion, we decided that we were doing the right thing by fixing the place up. Maybe we were just fooling ourselves because we were having so much fun, but that's what we decided.

We had a room built for birthday parties, and we installed bumpers in the gutters of some lanes so little kids could have fun bowling without getting frustrated because they threw so many gutter balls.

We put in a snack bar, and hired waiters and waitresses to deliver food and drinks.

"Let's put 'em on in-line skates!" Squishy suggested.

"Yeah!"

Squishy and I were having a blast. We came up with a bunch of wacky ideas to get people excited about coming out for a night of bowling. We planned a Baldy Bowling Night, when anyone who came in with a bald or shaved head could bowl for free and get a free head waxing in Mr. Z's ball buffer.

We planned an Opposite-Hand Night, where lefties would have to bowl right-handed and righties would have to bowl left-handed.

We planned a Pitch-black Night, where people would compete to see who could bowl the best game blindfolded.

We planned to give out prizes for everything: high game of the day, low game of the day, most splits, goofiest bowling shirt, dirtiest car in the parking lot. Anything to get people out for a fun night of bowling.

"Hey, Ouch," Squishy said one night while we were sweeping up pieces of glass in the parking lot. "What if Mr. Z is right?"

"About what?"

"What if the world really *is* going to end on New Year's Eve?"

"You're not going psycho on me, are you?" I asked.

"I was just thinking that maybe Mr. Z might be the sane one and everybody else is crazy. That's the way it always happens. The crazy guy is always right and the normal people turn out to be the ones who were nuts."

"If the world is about to end," I said, "we sure have wasted a whole lot of time fixing this place up."

We kept sweeping the parking lot in silence for a while, and then Squishy came out with, "Hey, I was thinking, Ouch. You know what Bowl-a-Rama could really use?"

"What?"

"A new name."

I looked up at the big Bowl-a-Rama sign on the roof, which I had always taken for granted. I had always thought it was a pretty good name. But the more I thought about it, the more it sounded kind of old-fashioned. What did *rama* mean anyway? A new name would give the alley new life, new energy. And it would let people know the place was different.

We got permission from Mr. Z to change the name, and batted around a bunch of ideas. Bowl-a-Mania. The Parkfield Bowling Center. Strike Zone. Let the Good Times Bowl.

No, none of these were any good. We needed something different, something cooler, something that would grab people's attention.

Finally, Squishy snapped his fingers.

"How about—Extreme Bowling?" he suggested.

Extreme Bowling. Extreme sports were pretty hot, and it was a funny name, because bowling was just about as far as you could get from being an extreme sport. We both agreed that Extreme Bowling would be a cool name for a bowling alley.

We ordered a new sign with huge letters spelling out EXTREME BOWLING in all the colors of the rainbow. It was fun watching the sign get mounted on the roof. We ordered thousands of Extreme Bowling bumper stickers, balloons, napkins, and T-shirts.

Only a few weeks had gone by, but you couldn't even recognize the old Bowl-a-Rama anymore. People were starting to come by to see what all the excitement was about. Cars were slowing down and honking as they drove by. Word was getting around town that something big was going on where the old Bowl-a-Rama used to be.

Finally, on December twelfth, it was finished. We had created the coolest bowling alley in the world.

There was just one thing that bothered me. Every so often, while we were working, I would pull out that note Mr. Z had found on his windshield.

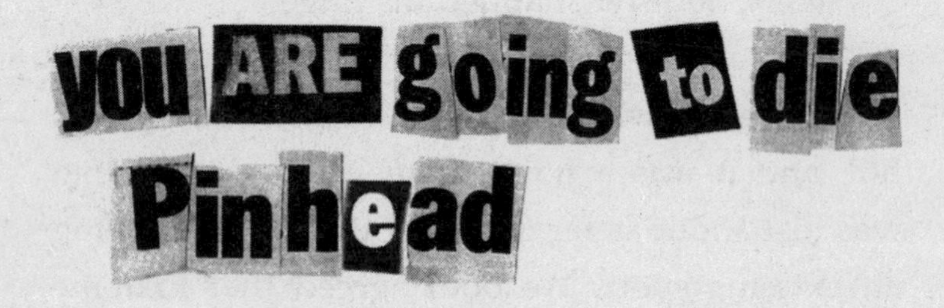

Who had put it there, and why? And why would somebody call Mr. Z "Pinhead"?

We had no other clues, and no other threats. Maybe it was just a practical joke. As the days went by and nothing bad happened, we put it in the back of our minds. But I still kept the note in my pocket, and every so often I would look at it.

CHAPTER 11

The Bowling Clown

Squishy and I had promised Mr. Z an End-of-the-World party, and we decided to throw him the bowling party to end all bowling parties. It may have been the final days of the world for *him*, but for us, it was the grand opening of the hottest and hippest bowling alley anyone had ever seen.

We told everybody at school there would be free hot dogs, pizza, and soda at Extreme Bowling on Friday night at seven-thirty. We put flyers up on every telephone pole in town. There was an article in the local newspaper and they were talking about it on the radio too.

By seven o'clock on Friday night, it was so crowded in Extreme Bowling that it was hard to move. It seemed like the whole town had come. Chief Strat and Mayor Little were there. Her term of office was coming to an end, but she was still pumping hands with every voter, out of habit. The guy who owned the bowling alley on Route 101 was there. My parents and Squishy's parents were there. I spotted that guy Herb Dunn who wanted to open up the dog bakery. Even Leslie King, that jerk who made fun of me because I liked bowling, was there.

It was the social event of the year. Squishy and I had spent the afternoon blowing up balloons and putting them all over the place. We hired a DJ, and some people were even dancing.

"Great party," Leslie King told me as he stuffed a hot dog in his face, "but you're still a dweeb, bowel boy."

"I'll take that as a compliment."

It was great watching Mr. Z walk around being congratulated by everybody. He almost seemed normal. That is, until he leaned over to me and whispered, "Let's enjoy this while it lasts. Two more weeks and all of this will be rubble."

We had strung a big red ribbon across all the lanes so that Mayor Little could cut it with scissors and officially declare Extreme Bowling open to the public. She and Mr. Z made their way to the microphone stand, which was in front of lane ten.

"Well, I must tell you," Mayor Little said as she looked around the place, "I am bowled over!" Everybody clapped and laughed. "It was less than a month ago that the town council and I seriously considered shutting this bowling alley down. But I think I speak for the rest of the council when I say that is not going to happen." More cheering. "You, sir, have done an outstanding job."

She handed Mr. Z the scissors and got out of the way so he could say a few words before cutting the ribbon. He tapped the microphone a few times nervously. Public speaking must have been new to him.

"Thank you, Mayor Little. But honestly, I had very little to do with all this. Those two young fellows over there, Ouchie and Squishy, did all the work. They're the ones who should cut this ribbon."

Everybody started yelling, clapping us on the back, and pushing us toward the microphone.

This was the moment I had been waiting for. I had been thinking about it ever since we had that talk with my mother about Mr. Z. I grabbed the scissors and the microphone before Squishy could get his grubby hands on them.

"Thank you, Mr. Zamboni," I said. "I'll be happy to cut the ribbon. But it would be only fitting if *you* were to roll out the first ball to open the new and improved Extreme Bowling. What do you say, everybody? Shouldn't Mr. Zamboni throw out the first ball?"

The crowd exploded in cheers. Mr. Z looked at me, panic-stricken. He shook his head no. I shook my head yes.

"Zamboni! Zamboni! Zamboni!" the crowd began to chant.

"*You* roll the ball and I'll cut the ribbon," he whispered to me.

"No," I replied. "I'll cut the ribbon and *you* roll the ball."

"I've never bowled in my life. You know that."

"What better time than now to start?"

"My perfect game will be ruined."

"Once you get past this, you can live your life!" I insisted. "You've got to get over your bowlaphobia!"

"Zamboni! Zamboni! Zamboni!"

Mr. Z wouldn't budge. I was glad when Squishy

leaned toward us. He always knew the right thing to say to Mr. Z.

"What difference does your perfect game make now?" he asked Mr. Z. "The world is going to end in two weeks, right? I thought you said you wanted to go out with a bang."

"Zamboni! Zamboni! Zamboni!"

"It's your destiny, Mr. Z," Squishy whispered.

Mr. Z took a deep breath and pulled out a handkerchief to mop his forehead.

"Okay," he said. "I'll bowl."

I cut the ribbon and everybody cheered. It became even louder when Mr. Z handed me his crutch and slowly limped over to the lane. Somebody handed him a bowling ball. He put his fingers in the holes and shook his head to let me know the fit wasn't right. Squishy got him another ball, which he liked better.

The crowd grew quiet when Mr. Z turned around to face the pins. He stared at them for a long time before beginning his slow, agonizingly slow and limping approach to the line. Finally, he brought the ball back and let it go.

It was the most pathetic roll I had ever seen in my life. Mr. Z was like one of those four-year-olds whose parents take them bowling for the first time and they throw the ball so slowly that it barely makes it down the lane. I felt bad. I desperately wanted Mr. Z to bowl and get over his bowlaphobia, but I didn't want him to make a fool of himself.

Funny thing was, though, he threw it right down the middle. The ball was rolling about one mile an hour, but it was heading straight for the head pin.

Everybody in Extreme Bowling stopped talking, eating, laughing, or whatever they were doing, so they could watch Mr. Z's ball inch its way down the alley, like a marble dropping through a jar of honey. The ball wasn't veering toward the gutter, like it usually does with a really slow roll. It just kept going straight.

"Looks good," Squishy said just as the ball tapped against the head pin slightly on its right side. The one pin toppled over slowly, like a tree that had been felled with an ax. It knocked over the two and the five pins. The two fell on the four pin, which took the seven down with it. The five pin landed between the eight and nine and somehow they both fell over. Meanwhile, the ball had been going so slowly that after it hit the head pin, it deflected slightly to the right, which is where the three pin was. It wobbled a little, and then it fell over to the right, like a drunk who had one too many. It landed on the six pin, which also went down, and by some miracle, took the ten pin with it.

For maybe a second, there was absolute silence. It was so quiet, well, you could hear a pin drop.

"Strike!" I shouted into the microphone. "He threw a strike!"

Nobody heard me, because the place was going nuts.

"I am still perfect!" Mr. Z shouted, raising his hands in the air. "It is my destiny!"

After Mr. Z's unlikely strike, the party only got better. We turned off the overhead lights and turned on the disco ball and the multicolored laser beams. The DJ cranked up the volume. The lanes filled with happy bowlers.

Everyone was having a great time. I had hired some jugglers who claimed to be able to juggle bowling pins and bowling balls, and they were actually doing it. A fat clown who was wearing a giant bowling pin where his head would be was dancing around and singing with a bunch of happy little kids.

"This is the greatest night of my life," I hollered so Squishy could hear me over the thumping music.

"You know what would be cool?" Squishy said. "If a homicidal maniac suddenly showed up and went berserk right now."

"Yeah, real cool, Squishy."

Right after I said that, out of the corner of my eye I noticed the fat clown with the bowling-pin head walking down the middle of lane ten. We had just waxed that lane in the morning, and you're not supposed to walk on the wood. Squishy noticed him too.

"Excuse me, ladies and gentlemen," the clown announced. "Excuse me for one moment. . . ."

He must have had some kind of microphone system in his clown costume, because we heard every word he said, even though I couldn't identify his voice. The DJ turned the the music down.

"My name is Pinhead the Bowling Clown," said the clown. "Can everybody here say 'Pinhead the Bowling Clown'?"

Squishy turned to me.

"I didn't hire any clown. Did you hire a clown?"

"I didn't hire a clown either."

"I thought you hired the clown."

"I thought *you* hired the clown."

"Pinhead the Bowling Clown!" everybody yelled.

"Can't *hear* you!" Pinhead the Bowling Clown said, cupping one hand to his ear.

"Pinhead the Bowling Clown!"

"Wait a minute!" Squishy said. "Remember that note on Mr. Z's windshield?"

I pulled the note out of my pocket.

you ARE going to die
Pinhead

"He wasn't calling Mr. Z a pinhead!" I exclaimed. "He was signing his name to the note!"

"That's the guy!" Squishy exclaimed. "That's Pinhead!"

"We've got to stop him!"

We tried to push our way through the crowd,

but it was impossible. There were just too many people.

"I hope you're all having a good time tonight," Pinhead told the crowd, "because now you are all going to *die*!"

Pinhead reached inside his clown costume and pulled out a bowling ball. Only it wasn't a regular bowling ball. There was a string sticking out of it. Pinhead pulled out a lighter and lit the end of the string. It threw off sparks as the string got shorter.

"It's a bomb!" some lady screamed.

"Pinhead is an *evil* clown!" a kid yelled. "Run for your lives!"

It was pandemonium. Kids started crying. People started sprinting for the exits, screaming for their wives and boyfriends. Somebody knocked over a cart, and popcorn went flying everywhere. People were trampling each other.

Calmly, Pinhead walked up to the line at lane ten, brought his arm back, and rolled his bowling-ball bomb down the alley.

CHAPTER 12

The Suspects

"It's all my fault," Squishy said, holding his head in his hands. "I could have stopped it. I *should* have stopped it."

It was Saturday, the day after Pinhead had tried to blow up Extreme Bowling. We were sitting in our kitchen with my mom. The newspaper was on the table in front of us. The front page headline read

TERRORIST CLOWN SPOILS BOWLING ALLEY REOPENING

"Don't be silly," Mom said, patting Squishy's head. "There was nothing you could have done."

"Clowns are *always* evil," he moaned. "I should have seen it coming. There was a crazed clown in the movie *Funland*. And in *Carnival of Souls* too. In every movie with a clown in it, the clown is evil. Clowns, dolls, and puppets. You can't trust them. I should have known. I could have done something. How could I have been so stupid?"

"Stop kicking yourself, Squish," I said. "At least nobody was hurt."

We were thankful for that. When Pinhead rolled his bowling-ball bomb down the alley, it rolled over the fuse and snuffed itself out. The ball went into the gutter and rolled harmlessly into the ball return. A few people were bruised and scraped in the mad dash for the exits, but there were no serious injuries.

Once everybody was safely out of the building, Chief Strat called in the bomb squad to investigate, and they told us that the ball Pinhead rolled was basically eight pounds of dynamite. If the thing had exploded, it might have blown up a good part of Extreme Bowling and killed a lot of people too.

In all the confusion, Pinhead managed to take off his clown costume and blend into the crowd running for the emergency exits. The police searched everywhere and questioned a lot of people, but they never found him.

"We were so worried that Mr. Z was a psycho,"

I said, "and the whole time there was *another* psycho running around loose in Parkfield."

"That always happens," Squishy said, shaking his head. "I should have known. I let down my guard."

After this, Squishy was completely convinced that we were characters in a horror movie. We were in the middle of it now, he insisted. There would be some big confrontation with evil at the end of the story. He wasn't sure which one of us was the main character, but he was sure that the other one was going to die a horrific and painful death.

"Don't be silly," my mom said. "There was no way anyone could have predicted that a psychotic clown with a bowling-pin head would try to blow up the bowling alley. The important thing now is to figure out who this Pinhead lunatic is and let the police take care of him."

"What makes you so sure it's a him?" I asked. "Women can be psychos too."

"He had a man's voice," Mom pointed out. She notices everything.

My mom loves it when she gets the chance to use the psychological skills she picked up in college. She suggested we sit down with paper and pencil and draw up a list of suspects from the people we knew were there when Pinhead attacked. Then we'd try to figure out which one had the motive and the means to carry out this heinous attack.

I thought it was a pretty good idea. The only problem was that so many people could have done it. Mom gave Squishy the pad, and this is what he wrote:

POTENTIAL PRIME PINHEAD
PERPETRATORS

LESLIE KING. The jerkiest kid in school.

-MOTIVE: He hates Ouchie for some reason and may want to do him harm. He hates bowling too, and is just enough of a juvenile delinquent to want to blow up a bowling alley.

-PSYCHO? Possibly. Or he may be just a jerk.

-ON THE OTHER HAND: He may be completely innocent, and he might end up being Pinhead's first victim. The obnoxious jock is usually the first to go.

CLIFF DWELLER. The guy who owns Bowl Drome on Route 101.

-MOTIVE: Wants to see Extreme Bowling fail, because if it succeeds, it will take business away from Bowl Drome. Got up at town meeting and said he wanted Bowl-a-Rama condemned.

-PSYCHO? Don't know him well enough to tell. But he has shifty eyes, and all psychos have shifty eyes.

-ON THE OTHER HAND: Ouchie's mom says he seems like such a nice man, and that you can't convict a guy of committing a crime because he has shifty eyes. Too bad, I say.

GAZEBO ZAMBONI. Cannot rule him out just because he owns Extreme Bowling.

-MOTIVE: Blowing up his own bowling alley might just be his idea of "going out with a bang."

-PSYCHO? He's prays to bowling balls, sees ghosts, and thinks the world is going to end in a few weeks, so he's certifiably crazy.

-ON THE OTHER HAND: We didn't see Pinhead limping and Mr. Z has a limp.

-ON THE OTHER OTHER HAND: Maybe Mr. Z was faking his limp the whole time so nobody would suspect he was Pinhead.

HERB DUNN. The dog baker.

-MOTIVE: He stood up at the town meeting and said he wanted to open up a dog bakery on the site of Extreme Bowling.

-PSYCHO? Anybody who would want to open up a bakery for dogs must be a psycho.

-ON THE OTHER HAND: Animal lovers don't usually resort to violence.

POLICE CHIEF STRAT.

-MOTIVE: Ouchie thinks it's ridiculous to suspect the Chief of Police of committing a crime. But I told him about a dozen horror movies in which that was exactly what happened.

-PSYCHO? Possibly. Psycho loonies are often the person you least suspect.

-ON THE OTHER HAND: He has a sworn duty to uphold the law, not to break it.

OUCHIE'S DAD.

-MOTIVE: He doesn't like bowling and resents the fact that Ouchie likes bowling better than football.

-PSYCHO? Not known for psychotic acts, except for the time that chipmunk got in the house and he ran around chasing it with a shovel.

-ON THE OTHER HAND: Why would he try to blow up a place when his wife and son were in it?

GOTTFRIED SCHMIDT'S GHOST.

Cannot rule him out just because he's dead.

-MOTIVE: He could be angry because of all the changes we made to the bowling alley. And ghosts always like to make trouble for the living because they're jealous of us.

-PSYCHO? Possibly. All inventors are tortured geniuses, and most tortured geniuses go nuts at some point in their life. Or, in this case, after their life.

-ON THE OTHER HAND: The only one who has actually seen him is Mr. Z, who is a psycho himself.

MY BROTHER, Ronnie. Because he's stupid and annoying and I hate him.

That was our list of suspects. Well, there were two more, actually. After Squishy was finished, I added:

SQUISHY. For two reasons. First, because he put my dad on the list of suspects, which was really mean. Second, Squishy might be Pinhead because he was constantly saying how cool it would be if a psycho went berserk, but no psychos have ever gone berserk in our town and he *got tired of waiting for one of them to go berserk.*

And then Squishy added one more name to the list.

<u>OUCHIE</u>. Because it's not fair that I'm a suspect and he's not.

We could have added a few more names, but we ran out of paper. Besides, at that point my dad burst in the front door. He came running into the kitchen like he was having a bathroom emergency.

"Did you hear the news?" he said, all out of breath.

"What news?" Mom asked.

"Somebody tried to burn down Bowl-a-Rama!"

CHAPTER 13

Pinhead Strikes Again

Squishy and I were on our bikes before my dad finished the sentence. We were imagining the most horrible scenarios. . . .

Flames engulfing the splintered remains of Extreme Bowling. Smoke curling off blackened bowling shoes. Poor Mr. Z trapped inside the burning wreckage, clinging to the first automatic pinspotter.

When we got there, fortunately, the building was still standing. So was Mr. Z, who was out in the parking lot surrounded by Chief Strat, reporters, and a few curious bystanders.

"What happened?" we asked one of the reporters.

"Pinhead," was all he said.

Chief Strat said it was safe to enter the building

again, and Mr. Z invited Squishy and me inside. We had missed all the excitement, apparently. The cops and reporters and everybody else went home.

It turned out that somebody had climbed up on the roof of Extreme Bowling and tied a hot-air balloon up there. The balloon was shaped like a bowling pin, and it was about three stories high. The thing was floating up there for a few hours, and people had assumed it was just some advertising gimmick for the bowling alley.

"Have you ever heard of the *Hindenburg*?" Mr. Z asked. We hadn't, and he told us it was this gigantic passenger Zeppelin that had caught fire back in 1937 and killed a bunch of people who were riding it.

Pinhead must have been thinking about that, because a witness spotted somebody shooting a flaming arrow at the floating bowling pin. He must have been trying to ignite the gas-filled balloon and create a huge fireball that would land on top of Extreme Bowling and burn the place down. Pretty inventive, I had to admit.

The only problem was that as soon as the arrow left the bow, the flame went out. All the arrow did was puncture the balloon. The helium rushed out of the hole and the thing deflated. It floated down and landed gently on the roof. The police came and evacuated the building just to be on the safe side.

"How can you be sure it was Pinhead?" Squishy asked.

Mr. Z showed us a note that was left outside police headquarters. It was stuck inside one of those cardboard tubes that comes inside a roll of toilet paper. . . .

Pinhead strikes Again! Nobody Will be SpAREd!

Even though he fully believed the world was going to end, and even though he felt everything came down to fate, Mr. Z looked pretty shaken up. He expected to die in a few days, but he wasn't expecting that somebody would try to *kill* him. He wanted to catch this psycho Pinhead just as much as we did.

After the second attempt to destroy Extreme Bowling, Squishy and I decided to go to Chief Strat and see what was being done to catch Pinhead. We rode our bikes over to Police Headquarters and asked to speak with him.

"Do you boys want lollipops?" was the first thing he said to us, holding out a candy jar that was on his desk. I took it as an insult. I'm not six years old. I wanted to be taken seriously.

"No thank you," I said.

"I'll have a lollipop," said Squishy.

"We want to know how the investigation is going," I said, lowering my voice a little so I'd sound more grown up.

"What investigation?"

"The investigation of Pinhead the Bowling Clown," I said, trying to hold down my anger.

"There is no investigation," Chief Strat told us. "No crime has been committed."

"What do you mean?" Squishy said, taking the stupid lollipop out of his mouth. "He rolled a ball of dynamite down the alley! He tried to set off a gas bomb on the roof! That sounds like criminal activity to me!"

"Boys, boys, boys," the Chief said, with a little

chuckle. "You've got a lot to learn about the criminal justice system. You see, the problem is that nobody was hurt. If nobody was hurt, nobody made a complaint. And if nobody makes a complaint, I have no crime to investigate."

"Let me get this straight," Squishy said. "You're saying that it's a *problem* that nobody got hurt?"

"From the police standpoint, yes."

"So you have to wait until somebody is hurt or killed before you can do anything?" I asked.

"Now you're catching on," he said. "Boys, what we're dealing with here is the most devious and difficult kind of criminal to arrest."

"What kind is that?" Squishy asked.

"The incompetent kind," the Chief said. "This Pinhead was smart enough to construct a bomb, but he couldn't set it off. He was smart enough to rig up a giant flammable balloon, but he couldn't ignite it. Pinhead's genius lies in his incompetence. As long as he fails, we don't have a case. What we're dealing with here is very possibly an idiot."

Squishy leaned over to me and whispered in my ear, "That's for sure."

"Isn't there *something* you can do?" I begged.

"We were lucky the first two times. Chances are that Pinhead is going to keep trying to destroy Extreme Bowling."

"I wish I could help you, boys. Feel free to take a lollipop on your way out."

Now I was really mad.

"No thanks," I said, getting up to leave. "I never take candy from strangers."

"Maybe if we're lucky, Pinhead will murder somebody next time," Squishy said. "Maybe *then* you'll launch an investigation!"

We were just about to storm out of there when Chief Strat's secretary ran in.

"Chief Stratocaster," she said, "there's been a murder!"

CHAPTER 14

The Root of All Evil

Chief Strat, for probably the first time in his life, looked like he meant business.

"Who's been murdered?" he snapped, pounding his desk with his fist.

"A man named Herb Dunn," said his secretary.

"Who the devil is Herb Dunn?" he asked.

"I remember that name," Squishy said. "Herb Dunn is that guy who wanted to start a dog bakery."

"Why would anyone want to kill him?" I asked.

"Maybe his dogs did it," Squishy guessed. "They were probably sick of eating his homemade dog food."

"He was poisoned," the secretary said. "He was taste-testing one of his doggie muffins, and it was laced with arsenic."

"Well, I guess the dogs are off the hook," said

Squishy. "The guy shouldn't have been eating dog food anyway."

"I guess Herb Dunn is off the hook too," I said. "If Pinhead killed him, he can't be Pinhead."

"That's *if* Pinhead killed him," Squishy said.

"You two kids need to get out of here," Chief Strat told us. "This is no place for children. I have a murder investigation to, uh . . . investigate."

"I say Police Chief Strat is our murderer," Squishy said, pacing back and forth on the rug at Extreme Bowling in front of me and Mr. Z. "Maybe he didn't want to help us catch Pinhead because he *is* Pinhead!"

"How could he be Pinhead?" I asked. "He was sitting there when he got the news of the murder."

"That was his alibi," Squishy told me. "He didn't do the actual poisoning. He paid somebody to do it for him. Murderers do that all the time."

"I don't think it was him," Mr. Z said. "I've known the Chief for years. Even though he wants to shut my place down, he's not a murderer."

"Well, I know one thing," Squishy said. "Chief Strat is a moron. He couldn't solve a murder if the killer was standing there with a bloody knife in his hand. If we're going to catch this Pinhead psycho, we're going to have to do it ourselves."

"How?" asked Mr. Z. "He can attack at any time, in any way."

"Well, what evidence do we have?" I asked.

We didn't have any information on the dog-bakery guy, but we made a list of evidence we *did* have. An unexploded bowling-ball bomb. A giant plastic balloon in the shape of a bowling pin. No fingerprints on either of them. There were two notes from Pinhead, but no handwriting. There were lots of witnesses to the first attack, but nobody saw Pinhead put his costume on or take it off. No photos. No video. No audiotapes. We had no DNA evidence, and even if we did, Chief Strat probably wouldn't help us test it. Especially if *he* was Pinhead himself. It wasn't like we could bring in forensic experts and crime-scene investigators. We didn't have much to go on.

"Maybe we can set a trap," I suggested.

"Yes!" Squishy said. "Maybe we can make Pinhead attack when we *want* him to attack."

"What kind of a trap?" Mr. Z said.

"We've got to give him an irresistible target," Squishy said.

"The target is the bowling alley," Mr. Z said. "He wants to destroy the place, and hopefully kill a lot of people in the process."

"We've got to get the whole town out here again," I said. "That will tempt him."

"I don't see that happening," Mr. Z said. "Folks are scared to come here now. They don't want to be here the next time Pinhead pulls one of his crazy stunts. I mean, face it, boys. Bowling is fun, but it's not worth risking your life for."

"There must be a way we can fill Extreme Bowling again," I said. "Then we can swoop in and capture Pinhead before he can strike."

That's it!" Squishy exclaimed, snapping his fingers. "You said it!"

"Said what?"

"Strike! We can hold a contest. We'll give one person a chance to roll a ball, and if they knock down all the pins they win something. A free pair of bowling shoes, or whatever."

"I don't know about you," I said, "but I'm not risking *my* life for a pair of bowling shoes."

"Money," Mr. Z said. "It's got to be money. The biggest motivator on earth. The root of all evil. The almighty dollar."

"We'd have to give away a lot of those dollars to attract a crowd," Squishy said.

"You think a million would do it?" Mr. Z asked, raising one eyebrow.

We both looked at him. He couldn't possibly be thinking of giving away a million dollars. I mean, the guy was crazy, but nobody was *that* crazy.

"A million dollars," Mr. Z said. "It's a magical number. Even today, when you hear about all those athletes and rock stars earning all that money, there's something about a million dollars that sounds magical. People figure that if they only had a million dollars, it would solve all their problems. Believe me, people will risk their lives for it."

"The whole town would come out," Squishy said excitedly. "We could pick a name out of a hat or something. If they roll a strike, they win a million bucks. Anything less, and they get nothing. With the whole town there, Pinhead is sure to show. It's a foolproof plan."

"Gee, I don't know," I said. "A guy was just murdered. Is this really a good time to be holding a contest?"

"There's no better time," Squishy insisted. "It's the only way to catch Pinhead."

"I've got a million dollars in my wallet," Mr. Z said, jerking his thumb toward the safe in the back. "I don't mind giving it away. The world's going to end on New Year's Eve anyway. What difference would it make? We're all going to be dead. Might as well make somebody happy for a few days."

"We can't let you do that!" I protested. You've already spent a fortune fixing this place up. Giving away a million dollars is too much."

"I can't take it with me," Mr. Z said.

"What are you worrying about, Ouch?" Squishy said. "Mr. Z isn't going to have to give away a dime."

"How do you figure that?"

"Well, the average pro bowler throws what, about six or seven strikes a game? That's about fifty percent. He gets a strike half the time. Now take an amateur who might average 120 or 130. He probably throws one or two strikes a game, if he's lucky. So maybe ten percent of the time he throws a strike. Now imagine this place is filled with people yelling and stamping their feet. The guy—or girl—gets no warm-up. No practice. The pressure will be intense. I'd bet that person would have about a one percent chance of striking. The risk is minimal."

Squishy made a good point.

"Tell you what," Mr. Z said. "If you're worried about me and my money, schedule the contest for the night of January first. That's the day after the world is going to end. There won't even *be* a Million Dollar Strike."

The Million Dollar Strike. It had a nice ring to it.

CHAPTER 15

The Day the World Didn't End

The murder of the dog-bakery guy went unsolved. There was a lot of talk around town about who had done it and why, but nobody was arrested, nobody confessed, and everybody wondered. Everybody but the killer, that is.

We don't get much of a winter in California. When I woke up on the morning of December 31, the sun was shining and birds were chirping outside my window. There was no school. It certainly didn't look like this would be the day that the world was going to end.

But that's what the ghost of Gottfried Schmidt had told Mr. Z: New Year's Eve. No doubt about it. Mr. Z didn't know if it was going to be an alien invasion or a natural disaster or maybe a meteor that would strike the planet and wipe out all life forms. But one way or another, our planet would cease to exist sometime on December 31. That's what the ghost had said.

"We'd better get over to Extreme Bowling early," Squishy said over the phone while I was eating breakfast.

"Very funny. How come?"

"There's no telling what Mr. Z might do," Squishy said. "If you were totally convinced that the world was going to end sometime today, wouldn't you do some crazy things while you still had the chance?"

As usual Squishy made perfect sense. We biked over to Extreme Bowling, where we found Mr. Z pacing slowly back and forth near the bowling-shoe rentals. He had a handkerchief in his hand and he kept mopping his shiny head with it.

"Are you okay, Mr. Z?" we asked.

"As well as can be expected," he said, glancing up at the ceiling.

"Did Gottfried Schmidt's ghost show up last night?" Squishy asked.

"No. But today is the day. New Year's Eve. I'm sure of it."

We couldn't be bothered with that nonsense.

The world might end within twenty-four hours, but we had the *next* day to worry about. There was a lot of preparation that had to be done for the Million Dollar Strike contest.

We had to put out chairs for all the spectators to sit on. We had to make sure the left and right of each pair of bowling shoes matched up. We had to scrape the gum off the floors and empty the trash cans. We had to make sure the bathrooms were clean and stocked with plenty of soap and toilet paper. So many little things.

We had done a pretty good job of spreading the word about the contest, but just to be sure, Squishy had printed up a bunch of flyers on the computer that morning.

YOU COULD WIN A

MILLION DOLLARS!

Start the new year off right! Come to Extreme Bowling Thursday night, January 1. One lucky bowler will get the chance to roll ONE ball. A strike wins a million dollars—cash. This is for real. Be there or be square!

We rode all over town putting them up in every store window we could find.

"You're wasting what little time you have left," Mr. Z said when we got back. "There isn't going to be any Million Dollar Strike contest *tomorrow.* There isn't going to be any tomorrow."

He was so sure of himself, I almost started believing the world was going to end myself. I called my mother on the phone just to say hi.

In the back of our minds, of course, was Pinhead. He was the whole reason we were having the Million Dollar Strike contest in the first place. We had to catch him before he was able to do anything violent. But who knew what he might try? He was inventive, that was for sure. What evil plan would he be hatching now?

After lunch, we called Chief Strat to remind him about the Million Dollar Strike contest. If he was Pinhead, we wanted him to show up. If he wasn't Pinhead, we wanted him to *catch* Pinhead. Chief Strat suggested Squishy and I borrow cell phones from our parents and carry them with us so we could let him know the instant one of us spotted Pinhead.

Chief Strat told me he would have ten officers

stationed at Extreme Bowling, and they would be dressed in street clothes. He said he wanted the police to keep a low profile until Pinhead showed up. Then they'd nab him before he had the chance to hurt anybody. Ever since the murder of that Dunn guy, Chief Strat was much more cooperative.

Mr. Z became increasingly more agitated as the day went on and nothing bad happened. If the world was going to end, he told us, he wished it had happened in the morning. That way, he wouldn't have to spend the whole day thinking about it. He just wanted to get it over with.

Poor guy. It was sad watching him pace back and forth all afternoon, wiping the sweat off his glistening head. We tried to comfort him, but we didn't do much good. How was he going to handle it when midnight came and the world *didn't* end? I wondered. Everything he had ever believed in would be shattered.

It was Squishy's idea that maybe it wasn't safe to leave Mr. Z by himself that night. My parents were having a little get-together with some of their friends, and I really didn't want to go. Squishy and I called up our folks to get permission to stay at Extreme Bowling until midnight. My mom didn't feel entirely comfortable with me hanging around "that disturbed man." But I argued that Mr. Z was harmless and he needed us to babysit for him, so she said it was okay.

Rain started to fall outside during the afternoon. We could hear it hitting the roof. It began thundering too. Maybe the world was going to end in a flood, it occurred to me, like Noah's ark. But we didn't have an ark. All we had was a bowling alley.

Mr. Z ordered a pizza for us, and when it was delivered he shocked the delivery man by giving him a twenty-dollar tip. The guy had to drive through a thunderstorm, and well, after all, the world was about to end. You can't take it with you. Mr. Z got us sodas too.

"Do you think it's just a coincidence that a bowling strike and a clap of thunder make almost the exact same sound?" Mr. Z said absentmindedly as we ate. "Do you think it's just a coincidence that the earth and a bowling ball are the exact same shape? Or does it mean something?"

"Beats me," I said.

Mr. Z leaned back in his chair and munched a pizza crust. After being nervous all day, he looked like he was coming to accept his fate.

"Do you know what bedposts are?" he asked us.

"The posts on a bed?" Squishy said.

"Bedposts are what we used to call the seven–ten split back in the old days."

I had certainly had my share of seven–ten splits. That's when you leave the seven pin and ten pin standing at opposite sides of the lane. You don't want to do that. It's the only spare that's impossible to make. I always called it a "field goal" because it looks like a set of goal posts.

"I saw this guy once," Mr. Z said. "He was a portsider, a lefty. Tenth frame and he's down by eleven pins, so he's got to strike or spare. He's throwing a clean game up to this point. It's a big ball. He goes up there and hits the head pin on the Brooklyn side and he's staring at a set of bedposts. Game over, right?"

"Right," I say.

"Well, he goes right back up there and rolls his second ball so it nicks the seven on its right edge, bounces off the side and rolls all the way across the lane and knocks over the ten. Only time in my life I ever saw anybody make that split."

"So he won the game?" Squishy asked.

"Well, that's the funny thing," Mr. Z continued.

"Everybody in the whole place went bonkers when he made the seven–ten. He needed just two pins to win, but he was so jazzed that he doinked the last ball off his ankle and threw a poodle."

"Gutter ball?" I asked.

"Yep. Darndest thing I ever saw in my life. Funny game, bowling."

We talked bowling with Mr. Z late into the night. He didn't want to turn on the TV and watch the ball fall at Times Square. As it got closer to midnight, all we could do was sit there and watch the clock on the wall. Eleven-thirty. Quarter to twelve. Ten minutes to twelve. Five to twelve.

Then we were counting down the seconds.

Ten . . . nine . . . eight . . .

Up until the stroke of midnight, Mr. Z still thought the world was going to end.

Finally, it was twelve o'clock. There was some cheering and fireworks outside. But no alien invasion. No natural disaster. No meteor struck the earth and wiped out all life forms. We looked at Mr. Z to see what his reaction would be.

He still didn't believe it. He insisted that we walk outside. The rain had let up. We went out in the parking lot and looked up in the sky. It was filled with stars. Quiet and peaceful.

Mr. Z shook his head and we led him back inside Extreme Bowling. It had been a long, stressful day for him. He was exhausted from all that pacing and worrying. Squishy and I helped him to his bed. We took off his bowling shoes and tucked him in.

"See, Mr. Z," I said as Squishy turned out the light. "Everything turned out to be fine. The world didn't come to an end after all. There are no bowling ghosts."

But Mr. Z was already snoring.

Squishy and I had to go home and get some sleep too. January 1 was going to be a big day.

CHAPTER 16

The Lucky Number

Extreme Bowling opened for business at ten o'clock in the morning. But on *this* particular morning people were there long before that. When I arrived just before ten, the line was around the block.

It was ridiculous. People had come over right after their New Year's Eve parties had ended. Some of them had sleeping bags and tents and radios.

"The contest isn't until tonight," I told some guys who were playing cards on a cardboard box in the parking lot.

"We'll wait," one of them said. "We want to make sure we get a crack at that million bucks."

Mr. Z finally opened the front doors to let the crowd in. As each man, woman, or child entered, he wished them good luck and handed each of them a ticket with a number on it. Even Squishy and I took a ticket. He ripped the tickets in half and put one half into a big bucket. That seemed to be the fairest way to choose the person who would roll for the Million Dollar Strike.

Mr. Z had a big smile on his face. He looked years younger than he had the day before. Why wouldn't he be happy? Ten hours earlier, he had been pacing back and forth, absolutely convinced the world was about to end. And here he was, very much alive.

The only ones who were nervous now were Squishy and me. Our trap was set. The bait was in place. We were pretty sure that Pinhead would see a crowded Extreme Bowling as the perfect opportunity to strike. But we don't know when, and we don't know how.

We *did* know we were dealing with a psycho, and their brains don't work the same way the brains of normal people work. My mom told me that. There's no telling what that lunatic might try to pull off. We just had to wait and watch everybody.

"Your eyes are shifty," Squishy told me. "Are you sure you're not Pinhead?"

"Very funny."

"You know, I was right all along," Squishy said.

"About what?"

"This *is* a horror story, and one of us is the main character. We've been through the beginning. The middle is over. Tonight is the ending. Something horrible is going to happen tonight."

Maybe this whole Million Dollar Strike trap was a big mistake, I thought. What if Pinhead *did* attack? And what if he was successful and somebody was hurt or killed? Squishy and I would be responsible. It would be our fault.

Too late to worry about that now. It was like we had pushed a boulder down a hill. We couldn't stop it now if we tried.

As the place filled up with people who wanted a shot at the money and people who just wanted to bowl, I was doing my best to keep an eye on our prime suspects. They were all there. I spotted Cliff Dweller, the guy who owns Bowl Drome, playing pinball with some other guy. Chief Strat was there. Squishy's brother, Ronnie, was there. Leslie King, that jerk from school, was actually on a lane bowling with some of his moronic friends. I saw him heave a ball as hard as he could, straight into the gutter. Idiot.

"I thought you hated bowling," I said to Leslie after he took a drink from the water fountain.

"I do, bowel boy," he said. "But I like money."

We had to keep an eye on all of them, and everybody else too. It would be easy for anybody to sneak off into the bathroom, slip on their Pinhead costume, and come back out with a bomb or a machine gun or who-knows-what.

We should have installed surveillance cameras all over the place, it occurred to me. We should have had a metal detector at the entrance, like they do at airports. But then, if we had made the security too tight, Pinhead would just turn around and go home. We didn't want that either. We wanted to catch him, not scare him away.

The only person on our suspect list who hadn't shown up was my dad. That, of course, made him the new prime suspect. But I knew he had to go into work that night. I called him up, and he told me he would be over as soon as he could get away.

I really doubted that it was possible for my dad to be Pinhead. But you never know. As Squishy says, sometimes the evil forces of darkness might be right under your unsuspecting nose.

Oh, that dog baker, Herb Dunn, wasn't there either. Dead men don't bowl.

Seven-thirty. The crowd was starting to get restless. Pinhead still hadn't shown his face. Squishy and I vowed not to let down our guard for a second. We positioned ourselves at opposite ends of the lanes, watching the crowd at all times. I wondered where Chief Strat's police officers were. I couldn't tell. They were dressed in their regular clothes. Just as anybody could be Pinhead, anybody could be a police officer too.

Mr. Z stalled as long as he could, but eventually it was time to select the lucky person who would roll the Million Dollar Strike. He went out to lane ten carrying the big bucket filled with tickets.

"Ladies and gentlemen," Mr. Z announced, "this is truly a wonderful day for Parkfield and a wonderful day for the whole world. Mayor Little, would you honor us by randomly selecting the lucky winner of our Million Dollar Strike contest?"

Mayor Little came out of the crowd, waving her own ticket over her head.

"I hope it's me," she giggled, and everybody

laughed. "Folks, our Declaration of Independence promised each of us the right to life, liberty, and the *pursuit* of happiness. Not happiness, mind you, but the pursuit of happiness. Tonight, one of you will have the chance to pursue your happiness. Maybe you'll win a million dollars and use it to start your own business right here in Parkfield. Maybe you'll start a new life for your family. A million dollars may not make you happy, but it sure wouldn't hurt, right?"

Mr. Z held up the bucket of tickets so the mayor could reach in and pick one out. Mayor Little closed her eyes and stuck her hand in the bucket.

I scanned the crowd. *This* would be the perfect moment for Pinhead to come out with a flamethrower or anthrax or something.

Mayor Little pulled out a ticket and looked at it. Everyone stopped talking.

"The lucky winner is . . . number 8304!"

Everybody looked down at their tickets. *This* would be the perfect moment for Pinhead to attack, I thought. I put my hand on my cell phone so I would be able to dial 911 if I had to.

No Pinhead. No winner either.

"Repeat the number please!" somebody yelled.

"The number is 8-3-0-4," Mayor Little shouted.

I watched the doors. Pinhead *had* to show up now. He just *had* to.

Nobody had came forward with the winning ticket. Somebody in Extreme Bowling had to have it. Why weren't they coming forward?

A crazy thought crossed my mind. What if the person with the winning ticket was Pinhead? He might be standing here right now trying to decide if he should blow the place up or try to win the million dollars!

"Will everybody check the numbers on your tickets, please?" Mayor Little asked the crowd.

Oh, heck. I took my hand off the cell phone, just for a moment, so I could pull out my own ticket.

I reached into my pocket for it.

I pulled out my ticket.

I looked at it.

My number was 8304.

CHAPTER 17

The Million Dollar Strike

I couldn't believe it. This wasn't really happening. I looked at my ticket a second time just to be sure.

8304.

It was the winning ticket. I was the one who would get the chance to throw a strike for a million dollars. Me!

"I got it!" I shouted.

Everybody in the bowling alley turned and looked at *me.*

"Are you sure?" a lady standing next to me asked. I showed her the ticket. "He's got it!" she screamed.

A buzz started spreading through the crowd as each person told the person next to them who I was. There was cheering. There was whistling. People started clapping me on the back and pushing me toward lane ten. I don't think I was moving my feet consciously. Something else was propelling me forward.

"Ouchie! . . . Ouchie! . . . Ouchie!" people started chanting.

I was in shock. So many things were rushing through my brain at the same time. I hadn't prepared for this. I hadn't picked up a bowling ball all week. It never occurred to me that I would be picked to roll the Million Dollar Strike.

I hadn't even been thinking about bowling. All my attention had been on stopping Pinhead. Where was he? Maybe he wasn't going to come. Or maybe he figured he'd cross us all up. With everyone in town at Extreme Bowling, maybe Pinhead decided to rob or burn down all the houses in Parkfield. Who knew what sick ideas were going through his twisted brain?

That thought was pushed out of my mind by another thought. What if I rolled a strike? It was Mr. Z who had offered to put up a million dollars of his own money. But when he had made that offer, he thought the world was about to end and the money would be useless to him. The world didn't end. He would have to pay me a million dollars if I rolled a strike. And he had told me exactly how to do it.

I didn't want to take Mr. Z's money. We had already taken advantage of him when we tricked him into spending a fortune to fix up Bowl-a-Rama. But that had been for a good cause. We had saved the bowling alley. We had saved his *home*. The contest was just supposed to be a scheme to get people to Extreme Bowling so we could catch Pinhead. I never thought that Mr. Z would actually have to give a million dollars away. Mr. Z was my friend.

None of that mattered now. The crowd of people in front of me parted to make a path so I could get to lane ten. That's where Squishy and my mother and Mr. Z were standing.

"Ouchie! Ouchie! Ouchie!"

"You can do it, honey," my mother said, giving me a kiss on the cheek. "Just relax. I wish your father were here. He would be so proud."

"Ouchie! Ouchie! Ouchie!"

"You're not going to choke, Ouchie," Squishy said as he pounded me on the back and handed me a pair of bowling shoes to put on. "I know how difficult these pressure situations can be. You know you're gonna strike. You might as well just collect that million bucks right now."

"Ouchie! Ouchie! Ouchie!"

"Now, you remember everything I told you," Mr. Z said, putting an arm on my shoulder.

"I don't want to take your money, Mr. Z," I said.

"What's done is done."

Well, I decided, I was just going to go for it. There was nothing else I could do. I wouldn't miss on purpose, that was for sure. If I could roll a strike, the money would be mine fair and square.

You can do a lot with a million dollars. I could buy my own bowling alley if I wanted to. That would be cool. Bowling was my passion. I could even put a bowling alley in my house if I had a million dollars. And a snack bar! With pool tables and—

I told myself to stop thinking those thoughts. I was getting ahead of myself. If I could roll a strike, there would be plenty of time later to worry about how I would spend the money. For now, I had to focus on those ten pins.

"Ouchie! Ouchie! Ouchie!" People were screaming, stomping their feet against the floor.

"Hey, that's not fair!" somebody shouted over the noise.

I looked up and saw that it was Leslie King, that jerk.

"Ouchie works here! He should be disqualified! This contest was rigged!"

"He is not an employee of the bowling alley," Mr. Z announced. "He's an unpaid volunteer. And even if he were an employee, I never said employees were ineligible. So roll your ball, son, and give it your best shot."

"Ouchie! Ouchie! Ouchie!" The noise level in Extreme Bowling was incredible. The disco balls hanging from the ceiling were even vibrating a little.

Squishy handed me a bowling ball, the one he knew I used all the time.

"What about Pinhead?" I asked him. "Why do you think he hasn't shown up?"

"Let *me* worry about Pinhead now," Squishy replied. "You worry about knocking those pins down. That should be the only thing on your mind."

Squishy and everybody else backed off the lane to give me room. My palms felt moist. I wiped some sweat off my hand and held it over the blower to dry it off. I tried to put Pinhead out of my thoughts and focus on what I needed to do.

Ten pins.

Ten lousy, stinking, good-for-nothing, stupid pins. They were just standing there, taunting me, mocking me, daring me to knock them over. And I wanted to do just that. I *had* to do just that. For myself. For my dignity. More than anything else, for a million dollars.

I put my fingers in the ball and tried to remember all the advice Mr. Z had given me. Keep my arm straight and close to my body. Relax my grip on the ball. Bend my knee. Make sure my right foot didn't turn as I slid it toward the line. Follow through. So much to remember.

Mostly, I didn't want to embarrass myself. All I wanted to do was hit the head pin. If you don't hit the head pin, you can't strike. If you hit the head pin, at least you have a chance. With a little bit of luck, you'll get some action and the other nine pins will go down.

"Ouchie! Ouchie! Ouchie!"

People were cheering, chanting, stomping their feet so hard, it felt like the entire bowling alley was shaking.

I stared at the ten pins sixty feet away.

My heart was hammering in my chest. I took a deep breath.

I brought the ball up to waist level and began my approach.

One step. Two steps. Three steps.

I brought the ball back, slid my left foot forward, and kicked my right leg back for balance.

I rolled the ball.

CHAPTER 18

The Ending

There are only two possible conclusions for this story.

The obvious one is that I rolled a strike. When the last pin fell, everybody surrounded me with hugs and kisses. I was the hero. They picked me up and carried me around the alley on their shoulders. Mr. Z handed me the key to his safe and I was allowed to take out a million dollars. He still had plenty of money left for himself. We all skipped gleefully out of Extreme Bowling and everybody lived happily ever after. I was suddenly famous. I was on the cover of *Bowling Magazine*. I bought a bowling alley with the money. They made a movie about my life. I was a terrific main character.

Well, forget about it. That didn't happen.

The other possibility is that I knocked down

nine or seven or three pins or I rolled a gutter ball or whatever. I didn't strike. I was sad, of course, that I didn't win the million dollars. But it was still a happy ending and I was a great main character because my experience had taught me some valuable lessons about life, about friendship, about, oh, all that stuff people in stories always learn life lessons about. In any case, after all I had been through, I was a better person. Just as Mrs. Felice said is supposed to happen at the end of a story.

Nice try, but that didn't happen either. Not even close.

A third possibility would be for the story to end right here. But that would be just plain mean.

What actually happened was so amazing, so incredible, so unexpected that even now—three months after the fact—I can hardly believe this happened to me. If somebody told me they saw this in a movie, I wouldn't believe them. If somebody told me they read it in the newspaper, I wouldn't believe them either.

But it really happened, I swear it did. Do you want to know what happened? Okay, okay, I'll tell you.

CHAPTER 19

Extreme Bowling

When I released the ball, I knew it was going to be a good shot. Sometimes you just have that feeling when your fingers pop out of the holes. You know right away. I probably eased up on the power just a little bit for the sake of accuracy, but the ball was right in there, heading into the heart of the pocket between the head pin and the three pin.

Of course, as every bowler knows, throwing the ball right in the pocket is no guarantee that you're going to get a strike. Sometimes you roll a perfect ball and you still leave one or two pins. Other times you barely nick the head pin, but all the pins somehow scatter and fall. That's the mystery of bowling. When somebody gets a lucky shot, bowlers like to say, "Christmas came early this year."

In any case, it was out of my hands, in more ways than one. There was nothing more I could do to influence the path of the ball or how many pins were going to go down. I breathed a sigh of relief. It felt like a barbell had been lifted off my shoulders.

As the ball was heading down the lane, everybody in Extreme Bowling was *screaming*. It felt like the whole place was going to come down.

The ball took out the head pin and the three immediately. The two, four, and the seven went flying on the left side, as did the six and the ten on the right. The ball rolled through and knocked over the eight and nine pins.

The five pin was still standing.

But it wasn't over. Far from it. One of the other pins deflected off the side wall and skidded across the lane. It was bouncing right toward the five pin. It looked like it was going to take it out.

But it didn't. It stopped and rolled to rest against the standing five.

Mr. Z had warned me. No drive, no five.

A huge gasp of disappointment came out of the crowd, as if all the air had been sucked out of it.

For a millisecond, there was silence.

But then, the silence was replaced by a rumbling sound. Far away at first, and then louder, closer. It was the strangest thing. Nobody was stomping their feet anymore, but there was this rumbling sound. The disco ball hanging from the ceiling was shaking violently. For an instant, everybody just stood there, frozen.

That's when the emergency door slammed open. I turned and saw my dad run in from the parking lot.

"It's an earthquake!" he shouted.

The disco ball fell and shattered on the lane below it. The whole place was vibrating now. I turned around to see panic in everyone's eyes. All Californians who have experienced an earthquake know the look I'm talking about.

But then, astonishingly, they all started cheering and pointing behind me. Nobody cheers for an earthquake. I turned around to see what they were pointing at.

The five pin had fallen! The vibrations from the earthquake must have knocked it down.

"What's wrong with you people?" my father screamed. "It's an earthquake! Everybody get *out*!"

But before anybody could make a move, there

was a rustle of activity behind the snack bar. I turned around again, and this time I saw him.

Pinhead!

The stupid-looking clown with the bowling-pin head ran out into the lanes. He was holding a bowling shoe in each hand.

"I hate to spoil your little contest," Pinhead shouted. "But it's time for all of you to *die*!"

"It's Pinhead!" somebody shouted. "Get him!"

"Make one move and you're a dead man!" Pinhead shouted. "These are bowling-shoe grenades! I'll blow you all to kingdom come, and don't think I won't!"

"Run for your lives!" somebody shouted.

The floor was shaking and the walls were rumbling, and after that it was all confusion. People were screaming and diving for the exits. Pinhead pulled his arm back to throw one of his grenades, but before he could bring it forward, a big chunk of the ceiling fell on his pin head and he toppled to the ground.

I was frozen in place. The wood on the lane below me was splitting and splintering. The walls were starting to crack and give way. It looked like the whole building might come apart.

People were running everywhere. Parents were carrying babies. Girls were screaming and crying. This must be what it was like on the deck of the *Titanic* as it was sinking, I thought.

"I got our moms and dads out!" Squishy said, grabbing my arm. "Come on!"

"What about Mr. Z?" I asked.

"Forget about him!"

"We've got to get him out!"

We looked around frantically for a few seconds until we saw him. He was sitting behind the front desk, a calm smile on his face. We jumped over a fallen TV and ran over to him.

"Mr. Z!" I shouted. "We've got to get you out of here!"

"I *told* you the world was going to end," Mr. Z said calmly. "I was just one day off."

"The world isn't going to end!" Squishy said, "It's just an earthquake!"

"Oh, no. This is no earthquake. This is the *end* of the earth."

"*Please* come with us," I begged.

"I don't think so," Mr. Z said. "It was nice getting to know you boys. Thanks for all you did for me. But now I'm sure that this is my destiny."

A five-foot piece of the ceiling fell and crashed to the floor in front of us. The building was breaking up. If we didn't get out soon, we would never get out. We would have to leave Mr. Z inside.

"If you're going to stay here, at least give Ouchie the key to the safe!" Squishy told Mr. Z.

"But I didn't roll a strike," I protested.

"This is no time to argue about technicalities!" yelled Squishy. "The last pin fell down! That's all that counts. You won the contest fair and square. If he doesn't want the money, you might as well have it."

Another chunk of the ceiling came down to the left of us and shattered in a bunch of pieces.

"Squishy, forget it!" I said. "Let's just *go*!"

"Give him the key!" Squishy yelled.

Mr. Z reached into his pocket and pulled out the key.

"This must be *your* destiny," he said as he handed it to me.

We ran out of there, jumping over rolling bowling balls, dodging fallen arcade games and other debris.

Before we dashed through the emergency exit, I turned around for one last look. Mr. Z was gone.

We had just made it out the door and into the parking lot when we heard the horrible sound of bending steel. And then the outside wall of Extreme Bowling nearest to us started to move and buckle. It was leaning inward. Slowly it tilted until the weight must have been too great and it began to crumble. The roof and cinder block and concrete cracked and collapsed in a thundering crash that shook the ground and sent up a plume of dust that forced all of us in the parking lot to turn away.

The last thing I saw was the big neon Extreme Bowling sign. It flickered twice, and then toppled over in a crash of cracking glass and plastic.

And then it was over. Extreme Bowling was rubble.

CHAPTER 20

The Truth About Pinhead

For a minute or two, we all just stood there in the parking lot, stunned. It was impossible to believe that this place where I had spent so much time and loved so dearly was . . . a pile of junk. It had all happened so quickly.

The ground had stopped shaking and we didn't feel any aftershocks. It was over. My mom and dad ran over and hugged me and wouldn't let go for the longest time. Squishy's mom and dad were all over him too. We considered ourselves lucky to be alive.

Nobody who was standing there that night had ever experienced anything like it before, but everybody seemed to instinctively know what to do. The call went out for the emergency medical crew and the local fire department, in case there were explosions. The women started gathering blankets, food, water, and first-aid supplies. The men started digging through the rubble in case anybody could be pulled out alive. Everybody got out cell phones to call their loved ones and let them know they were okay before the story hit the news.

Chief Strat was walking around, barking out orders and asking people to move this way or that. It looked to me like he was putting on a little show for the TV news teams, which had already started arriving and were setting up cameras and microphones.

"We will hunt for survivors no matter how long it takes," he announced.

"Ouchie and I were the last ones out," Squishy told him. "There are only two people still in there—Mr. Zamboni and Pinhead."

"Nobody cares if Pinhead is dead or alive," I said, "but they've got to find Mr. Z."

From the looks of the rubble, it didn't seem like *anybody* could have survived. Tons of concrete and wood and steel had collapsed in a heap. Men were digging frantically through it all, but I was pretty sure Mr. Z and Pinhead were buried alive. We all stood around anyway, hoping. Nobody wanted to go home. I tried not to let anyone see the tears that were gathering in my eyes.

"Make way!" Chief Strat suddenly shouted after about thirty minutes of digging. "Give them room! We need a doctor, now!"

"They found somebody!" Squishy said.

The paramedics were coming out of the rubble with a stretcher. Everybody in the parking lot gathered around to see. I had to jump up and down to get any view at all.

"I hope it's Mr. Z," I said.

The paramedics had thrown a sheet over the body, I guess so nobody would be grossed out if it was really messed up. A doctor had made her way to the stretcher and she pulled back the sheet.

"It's Pinhead!" somebody shouted.

I jumped up to get a better look, and sure enough, Pinhead was lying there on the stretcher. His clown outfit had some blood on it and a dusting of ash, but the plastic bowling-pin head was still attached to the body. He wasn't moving. It was impossible to tell if he was dead or alive.

"Rip the head off!" somebody yelled. "We want to know who Pinhead is!"

"Yeah!"

The doctor refused to be rushed. She was leaning over Pinhead, checking for a pulse.

"He's alive," she said. "The plastic head may have saved his life, like a bike helmet."

Somebody handed the doctor a pocketknife. Slowly and carefully, she cut through the stitches that were holding the pin head and the clown suit together. She cut all the way around, and then, just as carefully, she lifted off the plastic pin head.

I knew it couldn't be Chief Strat, because he was standing there. It couldn't be Herb Dunn, because he was dead. It couldn't be my dad. It couldn't be Squishy or Ronnie or Leslie or me. It sure wasn't Gottfried Schmidt's ghost.

"It's Mayor Little!" somebody screamed.

I jumped up to catch a glimpse, and sure enough, it was Mayor Little lying there on the stretcher, her eyes closed. Gasps of disbelief went through the crowd as people spread the word that Mayor Little was Pinhead.

"Just as I suspected all along," Chief Strat announced. He held up the plastic bowling-pin head for the TV news cameras. "As you can see, there's a sophisticated electronic amplification device in the head that altered her voice so she would sound like a man. Very clever."

Squishy slapped himself in the forehead. "Of course!" he said. "How could I have been so stupid! Politicians are *always* liars and psychos!"

Mayor Little just lay there. The camera crews gathered around Chief Strat, and everybody made room so he could make a statement.

"This is a sad, sad day for Parkfield," he said. "I have been investigating the Pinhead case for some time now, and I suspected Mayor Little from the beginning."

"Chief, what made you first suspect the mayor?" a reporter asked.

"From the start, I thought Pinhead might be a woman," Chief Strat said. "The bowling-ball bomb she rolled down the alley weighed eight pounds. A man probably would have used a heavier ball, so he could do more damage. Also, Pinhead's second note was inside a cardboard toilet-paper tube. It is a well-known fact that men never change the roll of toilet paper. They leave it for their wives to change."

"Why would the mayor do such horrible things, Chief?"

"I can't speak for Mayor Little, of course. But as you know, she lost her bid for reelection in November. Her term is up on January 15. I know for a fact that she was bitter about that. Maybe she wanted to get revenge against all the people who didn't vote for her. And as mayor, of course, she had access to explosives. I looked into her background too. When she was younger, she won a medal for archery. Pinhead, as you know, tried to burn down the bowling alley using a bow and arrow."

"Was Mayor Little connected to the recent murder of the dog baker, Chief?"

"I believe so," Chief Strat said as he pulled an envelope out of his jacket pocket. "This letter was found in a search of her car just yesterday. It's from the Canine Cake and Cookie Company. Apparently the mayor was in negotiations to build a dog bakery on this site. That's why she wanted the bowling alley condemned. When this Dunn fellow came up with the same idea, she decided she had to get rid of him. I guess it's a dog-eat-dog world, so to speak."

The press conference came to a sudden end because the doctor had revived Mayor Little.

Now she was trying to restrain the mayor, who was flailing her arms around and moaning.

"I'm sorry I did it," Mayor Little cried. "I was desperate. I just wanted to start a new life after politics. Get rid of the stupid bowling alley. Open up a dog bakery and sell franchises all over the country. It was going to be like McDonald's, but for dogs. It was all going to be so perfect. So perfect."

"I hope you've got a good lawyer," Chief Strat said as he slapped a pair of handcuffs on Mayor Little. "Because you're going to need one."

It had been a long day, and a longer night. I wanted to stay there and search through the rubble for Mr. Z, but my folks told me the rescue crews would do all they could to find him. Reluctantly, I got in the car to head home.

I took one last look at the smoking ruins of Extreme Bowling. That's when I lost it. I couldn't stop myself from crying anymore and I just let it out. Mom and Dad said it was okay for kids my age to cry, especially in a situation like this when somebody close to you died. I felt so bad for Mr. Z. He may have been crazy and all, but he was a good guy. I resolved never to forget him.

And then, as my dad pulled out of the parking lot, I looked in the corner and noticed something very unusual.

The yellow Volkswagen Beetle was gone.

CHAPTER 21

Okay, the Real Ending

It took three months for the demolition company to clear away all the debris that had once been Bowl-a-Rama and Extreme Bowling. Every day Squishy and I would ride our bikes over there and watch the big earth-moving machines pick up the pieces and drop them into a dump truck to be hauled away. Every so often we would see a piece of something we remembered. The snack bar. The sound system. The sign. Little by little, the pile got smaller. It was sad to see our creation disappearing.

We got to know the workmen, and they didn't mind that we watched them. They knew how much it meant to me. And they knew what I was hoping they would find: some evidence of Mr. Z.

Squishy and I would sit around the parking

lot, guessing what happened to him. Maybe he got out alive and drove the Volkswagen down to Mexico or somewhere. Probably he was dead and the only reason his car wasn't in the parking lot was that somebody had stolen it. Who knew? Maybe he was hidden in one of those underground tunnels he'd told us about, on his hands and knees, praying to a bowling ball.

After three months of digging, there was nothing left to dig. The site was clear. It was as if Extreme Bowling had never existed. The workmen packed up their gear and told us how sorry they were that they never found the body of Gazebo Zamboni.

But on that last day of searching, they did find one thing that interested me: the safe.

When they found the safe at the bottom of all the debris, everybody in town got excited. There had been rumors that Mr. Z had kept dead babies and all kinds of other horrible things in that safe. People wanted to find out if the rumors were true. When Squishy and I announced that I had the key and that we'd seen the safe stuffed with money, everybody got even more excited.

There was some debate over what should be done with the contents of the safe. Mr. Z didn't have a wife or children, and he didn't even have a will. So whatever was in the safe was up for grabs. Some people thought that if it was filled with cash, that money should go to the town to improve the streets and public library and stuff. Some people thought the money should be donated to charity. I thought they should use the money to rebuild Extreme Bowling. Squishy thought at least a million dollars should go to *me*, because I had rolled the Million Dollar Strike, and Mr. Z had given me the key to the safe.

"I didn't roll a strike," I insisted.

"All ten pins went down," Squishy insisted. "To me, that's a strike."

Finally, the town council met and decided that if the safe was filled with cash, I deserved one million dollars of it and the rest of the money should go to the town budget to be used in case of another earthquake.

That Saturday, the safe was trucked over to the site where Extreme Bowling had stood. It was just one big vacant lot now. One last time, the whole town turned out. This time they weren't coming for free hot dogs and soda. There were no jugglers or entertainment. This time everybody in town showed up for one reason. They wanted to know what was in Mr. Z's safe.

A little platform had been built for the safe to sit on, and there were chairs for the members of the town council. There was a camera crew from the TV news too. Squishy stood next to me. My mother made me wear a tie and my nice shoes for the occasion, so of course I was totally uncomfortable.

Before they let me open the safe with my key, Chief Strat asked for a moment of silence. All the members of the town council got up and made a little speech saying what great guys Mr. Z and Mr. Dunn had been. They promised that Parkfield was going to get back on its feet again after the terrible tragedy. Everybody prayed for the rehabilitation of Mayor Little.

"This is so boring," I whispered to Squishy.

"Hey, don't complain. In five minutes, you're going to be a millionaire."

"Hey, Squish, I was thinking," I said. "You're my best friend in the world, right?"

"Right."

"We were in this thing together from the start, right?"

"Right."

"And I wouldn't be getting this money if not for you, right?"

"Right."

"Well, I was thinking it over, and whatever is in that safe, I want to split it with you fifty–fifty."

"For real?" Squishy said.

"Yeah."

"Can I get that in writing?" he asked, and I punched him.

Finally, it was time to open the safe. Chief Strat led me to the platform and wished me good luck. I took out the key Mr. Z had handed to me moments before Extreme Bowling collapsed.

Everybody stopped the conversations they were having. I slipped the key into the hole. It fit.

"Don't open that door!" Squishy shouted, and when everybody laughed, he added, "Just kidding!"

I turned the key and pulled open the heavy door.

The safe was empty.

Everybody gasped. My heart sank. My mom started crying. Squishy said a really bad curse word.

I put my head inside the safe, just to make sure it was empty. Upon closer examination, I found an envelope. In big, bold letters, it said, **FOR OUCHIE AND SQUISHY.** My heart soared.

I took out the envelope and held it up in the air for everyone to see. Some people started cheering.

"Maybe there's a *check* in there for a million dollars," Chief Strat said.

I tore open the envelope. There was no check inside. But there were a couple of sheets of paper stapled together. I read the first page silently.

January 1

Dear Ouchie and Squishy,

When I woke up this morning and saw that the world hadn't come to an end after all, I realized I had been wrong, wrong about so many things. Remember all those talks we had when I told you that everything came down to fate? Well, now I realize you were right. What happens to us is not determined by fate, and it's not determined by ghosts. It's determined by US. WE

are in charge of our own destinies.

Knowing that, I've decided it's time for me to move on. After the Million Dollar Strike contest tonight, I'm going to leave California and start a new life. I don't know where.

Remember how I always told you I might as well give my money away because you can't take it with you? Well, since the world didn't end after all, I decided I'm taking it with me. I just hope that whoever gets to take that Million Dollar Strike tonight is going to miss.

Thanks for everything you boys did to help me with my problems. You guys are great and I want to give you something to show my appreciation. You love bowling so much that I think you'll appreciate it. Enjoy!

Sincerely,

Gazebo Zamboni

I flipped the page over to look at what Mr. Z had given us.

It was the ownership papers for Bowl-a-Rama.

We were the proud owners of . . . absolutely nothing.

"What does the letter say, Ouchie?" somebody hollered.

"Yeah, what did he leave you?"

"It's personal," I said, and left it at that.

Squishy ran over to me to find out what was in the envelope. I showed him the letter. We were both pretty depressed about the whole thing. But Squishy does have a way of putting things into perspective.

"Look on the bright side, Ouch," he said. "What if you'd opened that safe and some grotesque fanged and clawed humanoid jumped out at you? Ever think about that? Or what if some mysterious dark power from the past was unleashed and we had to fight not only for our own lives, but for the lives of all humanity?"

"You know," I said, "I never thought of it that way."

"Hey, you know what would be cool, Ouch?"

"What?"

"It would be cool if right now some undead zombies showed up in the middle of the parking lot."

"Yeah?"

"Yeah, and world domination is their goal."

"Yeah?"

"Yeah, and their only source of food is gone and humans are the only prey left. And there's this big war."

"Yeah?"

"Yeah, and in the final conflict, only one species can survive."

"Yeah?"

"Yeah. Now *that* would be cool!"

"Yeah, real cool, Squish."

Well, that's the story. Beginning, middle, and end. I wish it had a happier ending. But then, you only see those happy endings in books. In the real world, sometimes endings are sad. Sometimes the hero doesn't get the girl. Sometimes evil wins. Sometimes a bowling alley gets destroyed by an earthquake, and you end up with nothing.

Mrs. Felice always tells us that the main character in a story always goes through some big change and learns something about himself that will make him a better person in the future. But what does she know? The only thing I learned was to keep my arm straight and close to my body. I learned to relax my grip and bend my knee and always follow through. I guess all I learned was how to be a better bowler. Nothing wrong with that.

But then something occurred to me. Maybe I wasn't the main character in the story after all. Maybe Squishy wasn't the main character either. Maybe the main character was Mr. Zamboni. He was the one who went through changes. He was the one who learned something about himself. He was the one who became a better person.

Maybe Mrs. Felice was right.